DIAMOND TAKERS

Other Lady Violet Mysteries:

Secret of the Crocodiles

Tiger Eyes

And for older readers:

Raspberries on the Yangtze

Climbing a Monkey Puzzle Tree

Wendy

The Unrivalled Spangles

to James

THE
LADY VIOLET
MYSTERIES

DIAMOND TAKERS

KAREN WALLACE

Karen Wallace

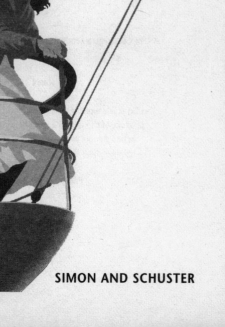

SIMON AND SCHUSTER

To Penny, with love and thanks

SIMON AND SCHUSTER

First published in Great Britain by Simon & Schuster UK Ltd, 2007
A CBS COMPANY

1 3 5 7 9 10 8 6 4 2

Simon & Schuster UK Ltd
Africa House
64-78 Kingsway
London WC2B 6AH

A CIP catalogue record for this book is available from the British Library

ISBN-13: 978-1-4169-0100-6
ISBN 10: 1-416-90100-0

Typeset in Garamond by M Rules
Printed and bound in Great Britain by
Cox & Wyman Ltd, Reading, Berks

ONE

Lady Violet Winters sat at a white wrought-iron table on the Boulevard Saint-Germain and watched as elegant young Parisian women strolled past in their sharply tailored suits, their hair cut in the new bobbed style.

Violet patted her long, curly black hair in a vague, frustrated kind of way. Usually, she wasn't interested in fashion. She left that sort of thing to her mother, Lady Eleanor, who regularly spent the morning choosing different outfits at some grand *costumier* and the afternoon wearing the ones that had just been delivered.

It wasn't so much the tailored suit or the bobbed

hair that had attracted Violet's attention – it was the style that somehow seemed to represent an independent spirit. Violet wanted her own independence and a proper education more than anything else. Not for her the silly finishing schools where girls learned how to do fine needlepoint, arrange flowers and win rich husbands. And it seemed to Violet that Paris was full of young women who believed exactly as she did.

Violet loved everything about Paris. From the moment she had stepped off the boat train at the Gare de Lyon late last night, it had been like entering a magical world.

Although it had been almost midnight, from the cab window she had seen the streets bustling with people as they shopped at stalls lit with strings of electric bulbs looped from lamppost to lamppost. Everything from flowers to books to canaries in cages was on sale.

It had been like driving through a carnival. And all the while, their driver had sung a love song at the top of his voice as they clip-clopped through the cobbled streets to the Ritz on the Place Vendôme.

'Vi! Look!' Now, at the table beside her, Garth

Hudson almost choked on his *melon glace* as he pointed down the crowded street.

Violet followed his gaze. She saw a man dressed in a top hat and tail coat, walking a leopard on a lead.

'Oh, boy,' groaned Garth in delight. 'This could only happen in Paris!'

They watched as the man and his leopard stepped to one side to let a grand lady in a ruffled lilac day dress and a grey feathered hat hurry past with three white poodles on gold leads. Both Violet and Garth had to hide their snorts of laughter as the terrified poodles took one look at the leopard and ran for cover under the lady's lacy train.

'*Whaddyathink*, Vi?' said Garth when he could speak without laughing. 'Will we find a mystery here?'

Violet grinned at the young American. Garth was her father's ward and had become an important part of her life. From their first Christmas together in Cairo, the two of them had fallen into solving mysteries that happened to turn up as they travelled around the world with her parents, Lord Percy and Lady Eleanor.

Violet swallowed the last of her own *melon glace* and nibbled at the bits of crushed pistachio that had been pressed together to form a rind. She raised her eyebrows teasingly. 'Maybe we should give up on the detective work and concentrate on sightseeing.'

'That would please your flatfish or whatever you call her,' said Garth, watching as an onion seller with at least twenty strings of onions hanging off his bicycle narrowly missed crashing into a cab.

'I call Madame "codfish", you numbskull!' Violet replied. 'When are you going to get it right?'

Madame Poisson was Violet's governess. It was the little Frenchwoman's whiskery face and popping grey eyes that gave rise to her nickname. Of course, Violet's mother, Lady Eleanor, would have preferred a more elegant, sophisticated governess for her only daughter, but Violet was fond of her dear codfish and refused to part with her.

'Talking about haddock heads,' said Garth, 'where did she say she was going?'

'To light a candle for her sister at Saint-Sulpice,' said Violet. 'Anyway, the longer she takes the better. My feet could do with another cup of hot chocolate.'

Despite their late arrival, Madame Poisson had been determined that Garth and Violet should see as much of the city as possible. So, straight after breakfast, they had walked all the way from the Place Vendôme to the Arc de Triomphe, stopping only briefly for lunch, then returned back through the Tuileries Gardens. Now, while Madame was away, they were sitting down for the first time that afternoon and Violet was glad she had worn her stout black patent leather boots and not the delicate red kid leather shoes her mother had suggested.

'How far do you think we've walked?' Violet asked Garth as the waiter set down two more steaming cups of chocolate.

'*Miles.*' Garth shrugged. 'I don't care. This is the swellest city ever.' He slurped his hot chocolate. 'Good chocolate, too. Better than London.'

Violet grinned. 'Better than New York?'

'Yup.'

Their eyes met. 'But not as good as Cairo,' said Violet.

'You got it.'

Across the boulevard, a cab stopped and a man and woman stepped down onto the street. Violet stared idly like everyone else did in Paris. The woman's face was fine-boned and her skin so white that the scarlet slash of lipstick she wore was almost startling. A thick swirl of blonde hair was bobbed to just above her jaw-line. Her suit was made of heavy black silk with a straight tapering skirt and a fitted jacket. A bright red beret was set at an angle on her head.

Violet turned to Garth to point the woman out but he was staring at her too. The man with her wore a striped single-breasted suit and a grey felt hat that made him look as stylish as his companion. They walked slowly and conspicuously across the boulevard and sat down at a table a little way away from Violet and Garth.

'Spies!' whispered Garth. 'Classy ones! On a secret mission from Constantinople!'

Violet's eyes gleamed. Making up stories about strangers was one of their favourite games. 'They arrived from Vienna, three days ago. An Austrian duke owes them a favour.'

'They recovered his priceless collection of Old Master drawings before they could be sold on to a ring of art thieves,' replied Garth.

'Who were hiding in a houseboat on the Danube!'

Now the man was leaning towards the woman with a serious expression on his face. From time to time, he crossed and uncrossed his legs and drummed his fingers on his lapel.

'What do you think they're talking about?' asked Garth as he sipped his chocolate.

The woman's face was hidden from Violet's view, but she could see that her gloved hands were clenched in her lap and that she was shaking her head as the man spoke.

'I don't know. It looks as if they are arguing about something.'

'I say we follow them,' said Garth. 'They look suspicious enough. We're bound to find a mystery.'

Violet turned back to her chocolate. She had been so caught up in their game that she had let the drink go cold. 'Aren't you forgetting something?'

'More of those little cakes you like?' Garth raised his hand to signal to a waiter. '*Garçon! Encore de petits fours, s'il vous plaît!*'

'Idiot!' cried Violet, laughing. 'I wasn't thinking about cakes! We're going to Monte Carlo tomorrow, remember? We don't have time to follow those people, no matter how suspicious they look.'

But Garth wasn't listening to her. He was watching the couple, who were now talking rapidly to each other. 'I bet they're plotting something,' he said. 'I'm going to listen in.' And, without waiting for a reply, he strode across to a table beside them and sat down, pretending to read his copy of *Baedeker's Handbook for Paris.*

The couple were so engrossed in their own conversation that they didn't even notice him. Suddenly there was a crash of breaking china and Violet turned to see a waiter bent over an upturned tray, staring furiously at a girl in a flowing purple coat who was moving clumsily between the tables.

At the sound of the crash, the mysterious couple rose like two startled birds and disappeared into the crowd.

'I was right,' cried Garth, running back to sit with Violet. 'They *are* plotting something!'

'What?'

'They're going to steal a diamond necklace!'

Violet's eyes widened. 'No! You must have misheard!'

Garth pulled up his chair and sat down. 'I'm sure I didn't! Listen! This is what they said—'

'Excuse me. I am Marie Cherkassky.'

Violet looked up to see the girl in the flowing purple coat standing beside their table. From her heavily accented English and her high, flat cheekbones, Violet guessed she was Russian. But before Violet could introduce herself in return, the girl sat down and began speaking rapidly in a high-pitched, excited voice.

'Of course, naturally, I am utterly beyond the pale and a complete nuisance! But you are English and that is what concerns me now.' Marie Cherkassky held out a plump, white hand. 'How do you do? I am of noble Russian stock, you understand, and destined to become –' she paused and looked from Garth to Violet '– a pianist of great renown. Already I am the prodigy.' Marie paused for breath and took the last *petit four* from the plate.

Out of the corner of her eye, Violet could see Garth's face darken and she almost burst out laughing. The so-called prodigy had just eaten the cake Garth had been saving for last. And it was obvious that he was annoyed not only at the disappearance of his cake with the mint icing but also at the interruption of his story. Violet, however, was more forgiving. In fact, she was fascinated by the Russian girl's complete disregard for social conventions. She held out her hand and said, 'I am Lady Violet Winters and this is Mr Garth Hudson from New York.'

She paused. 'Perhaps Miss Cherkassky would like a cup of hot chocolate, Garth.'

'Perhaps she would like some more cakes,' replied Garth. He turned as Marie wiped some crumbs from her mouth. 'They're real small, ain't they, Miss Cherkassky?'

Violet flushed with embarrassment, but Marie Cherkassky threw back her head and hooted with laughter. The possibility that Garth was irritated by her interruption had clearly not occurred to her.

'*They're real small, ain't they?*' she repeated delightedly. 'Now I practise my English *and* my American!' She squeezed Violet's wrist. 'Oh! How simply, beyond words, wonderful!' Then she lowered her voice and looked at them both with serious eyes. 'You know, I teach myself Latin and Greek in *six* months.'

'How very clever of you,' replied Violet, smiling. She was getting more and more interested in this strange girl, though she knew full well that when Madame Poisson returned, she would not be pleased to find Violet talking to someone she had never met before. The only thing to do was to get to know the eccentric Russian better and as quickly as possible.

'Tell me, Miss Cherkassky,' said Violet smoothly, 'how long have you been learning English?'

'No yet six months, Lady Violet, but that is not my concern.' Marie took a swift slurp from the cup of hot chocolate the waiter put in front of her. 'You see, I have taught myself from early years to concentrate on what is important at the now. And when I hear you speaking English, I say to myself, Marie, you are going to Monte Carlo and you are wanting to converse with dukes and duchesses without no embarrassings to help with the payings of the piano teachers. Now here is the chance to practise your English.'

'Monte Carlo!' cried Violet. 'What a coincidence!' She ignored Garth's scowling face. Even if he didn't like Marie, Violet did and the Russian girl would make a nice change from the usual brigade of dull duchesses' daughters Violet had been forced to visit on her last trip, two years ago.

'Why coincidence?' asked Marie, looking up quickly.

Garth tried to have a coughing fit but Violet pretended she didn't understand. '*We're* going there, too.'

'I *knew* it,' cried Marie. She touched her breast and

looked upwards. 'I *feel* these things.' She gazed into Violet's eyes. 'And I am *never* wrong.'

'Marie!'

A woman in a dark blue suit with a face like a porpoise and legs like tree trunks strode angrily down the boulevard towards them.

'Violette!' From the other direction, Madame Poisson was bustling through the crowd, her whiskery, pop-eyed face flushed and angry.

'Black curse be upon Tanenko,' cried Marie, looking quickly over her shoulder. 'That porpoise is my governess!'

The next moment both Madame Poisson and Marie's governess came to an abrupt halt in front of their table.

'My dear Madame Tanenko,' said Marie, as if nothing out of the ordinary was going on. She smiled at the grey face with the long snout that was trembling with outrage in front of her. 'How perfectly convenient of you to find me and my new friends.' She turned and gestured with her hand. 'Lady Violet Winters from England and Mr Garth Hudson from New York.'

'And may I introduce my own governess, Madame Poisson,' said Violet in the same voice. She smiled at her dear codfish. 'Marie Cherkassky and her governess, Madame Tanenko.'

Madame Poisson bowed to the young girl with the oddly grown-up expression and to the woman who looked like a porpoise. 'I am delighted to make your acquaintance, Mademoiselle Cherkassky, and yours, Madame Tanenko.'

Even though the two governesses exchanged looks of restrained friendliness, neither was in the least placated. This kind of behaviour was completely unacceptable. Madame Poisson could tell from the look on Garth's face that not only had this strange Russian girl forced herself upon them without a proper introduction but also that Violet was taken with her while Garth was not.

Thank goodness the young man has some sense! thought Madame Poisson, trying to keep her irritation with Violet from showing on her face. Heaven knows where the Russian might have come from!

'*Tiens!*' said Madame Poisson firmly. 'It is time to go back to the hotel. Come, Violette! We must return immediately.' She put her hand firmly through Violet's arm and pulled.

The firmness of Madame Poisson's fingers sent a surge of anger through Violet. What on earth was wrong with talking to someone of her own age? Who cared whether they had been formally introduced or not?

Violet could see that Marie was making no attempt to move, even though her own governess was speaking to her in insistent Russian and also pulling at her arm.

'Come, Violette!' repeated Madame Poisson.

Garth saw the stubborn clench of Violet's jaw and waited for her temper to explode. He didn't have to wait long.

'Really, Madame!' cried Violet, her cheeks burning. 'I would be grateful if you would allow me to exchange cards with Miss Cherkassky! We shall be staying in Monte Carlo at the same time and I should like to renew our acquaintance.' She fished in the little purse that hung from her belt and scribbled the name of the hotel her parents had mentioned on a visiting card. Then, pulling free from Madame Poisson's restraining hand, she stepped over to where Marie was standing and gave it to her. 'Do please call on us. I shall be delighted to help you with your English.'

Marie stopped in the middle of an angry exchange in Russian with her own governess.

'My dear Violet!' she cried. 'I will never again keep doubts that, to achieve greatness, I must follow my instincts!' She pressed the card to her lips. 'You are proof of it!'

'Amen to that,' said Garth under his breath.

Violet shot him a furious look but Marie beamed at him. 'Amen, as you say, Mr Garth Hudson. The gods are indeed kind!' Then with a deep bow, Marie took Madame Tanenko's arm and walked away.

'What an extraordinary girl!' declared Violet, ignoring Madame Poisson's furious face.

'What a pain in the butt,' muttered Garth.

'Really, Garth!' cried Violet crossly. 'Sometimes you are just so *American*!'

'You'd better believe it!' Garth looked at Violet and laughed. 'Oh, come on, Vi! She talked like a sewing machine and scared off those spies!'

'What spies?' demanded Madame Poisson. '*Bon Dieu!* I have hardly been away and you are 'obnobbing with strangers and worse! What next?'

Violet and Garth exchanged looks. There was an agreement between them that when things got sticky

15

with the codfish, it was Garth's job to win her round.

He was better at it than Violet could ever be.

'Madame,' said Garth, 'allow me.' He took the little Frenchwoman's arm and they walked along the boulevard. 'You are quite right, Madame,' he continued in his fluent French, 'we are not to be trusted. We will take *any* opportunity to get into trouble!' Garth gave the governess his most charming smile. 'Violet! We must apologise to Madame Poisson!'

Violet felt the remnants of irritation with her dear codfish disappear into the warm spring air. She kissed the little governess lightly on the cheek and winked at Garth over her head.

As soon as they got back to the Ritz, they would finish their interrupted conversation in private.

TWO

'So, what did you *really* hear those people say?' Violet asked Garth outside the hotel. Madame Poisson had left to go to her own quarters and it was the first chance they had had to talk alone since Marie had interrupted them on the boulevard.

The porter opened the heavy glass doors and they walked into the vast entrance hall. A huge chandelier spread sparkling light over heavy gold chairs positioned around sumptuous Turkish rugs. Lilies were arranged on the polished surface of every sideboard and the air was thick with their scent. The Ritz was unlike any hotel Violet had ever known. It was more like staying in a grand French château.

'So what—' began Violet again.

Beside her, Garth froze. 'Shhh!'

Violet turned and followed his gaze. 'It's them!' she gasped.

Sure enough, at the far end of the tiled marble floor, the man and woman who had been sitting on the boulevard were speaking rapidly to the manager of the hotel. They looked extremely upset. The woman's pale skin was flushed. She had taken off her red beret and kept running her hands through her short blonde hair. Beside her, the man they presumed was her husband drummed his fingers on his lapel as if trying to control his anger. A *gendarme* stood beside a skinny maid, who was wiping her face with a rag of a handkerchief and staring unhappily at her feet.

'Quick,' whispered Garth. 'We'll hear more from behind those palms!'

Violet and Garth hurried across the marble floor and sat down behind a clump of spiky leaves. As she watched Garth following every word of the conversation, Violet cursed herself for the hundredth time that day for not practising her French more often. Garth, on the other hand, was Madame Poisson's star pupil.

All Violet could do was stare at the couple and catch what words she could. But even she understood that the woman's diamonds had been stolen and that the maid had raised the alarm. At last the hotel manager turned to the *gendarme* and the two men left the hall, taking the maid with them.

Violet watched the woman's distraught face as she walked with her husband towards the wide, curving staircase. She appeared to be on the point of collapse. Then the two figures disappeared around a corner on the first floor.

'I must have misunderstood what they were saying on the boulevard,' said Garth before Violet had time to ask. 'They were planning to take a diamond choker to the bank for safekeeping – not planning to steal it.' He was furious with himself for getting it wrong.

'Was anything else taken?' asked Violet, feeling a twinge of pleasure at Garth's discomfort, since he was always teasing her for being so slack with her own French.

'Almost all of her mother's jewellery. She died last month and Madame Duchamps—'

'Who's she?' asked Violet.

'That's the woman's name,' explained Garth. 'She's called Florence and he's called Henri.'

Violet tried not to show that her moment of pleasure had turned back into irritation. *I must try harder with my French.* 'Did the *gendarme* have any ideas about who might have stolen it?'

Garth shook his head. 'That's why Monsieur Duchamps was so angry. He had heard a rumour at the British Embassy last night that there were jewel thieves in the city. But the *gendarme* didn't know anything about it.'

'What about the hotel manager?'

Garth shook his head again. 'He hadn't heard anything either. Otherwise, he said, he would have employed extra security guards in the hotel.'

Violet thought for a moment. 'Did the Duchamps inform the hotel that they had such valuable jewellery in their room?'

'Apparently they wrote a letter to the *concierge* but it was never delivered.'

'So what happens next?'

'The *gendarme* was sure that they would find the thieves soon. The choker is famous because of the pink diamond in the clasp, so it would be very hard to sell.'

'I wonder if the maid would talk to us,' said Violet. She couldn't bring herself to say 'you'.

'Uh-uh.' Garth shook his head. 'This is one mystery someone *else* will have to solve. Like you said on the boulevard, we're going to Monte Carlo tomorrow. And anyway, the Duchamps have offered a reward of ten thousand francs.' He paused and shrugged. 'That's a lot of money, even to a jewel thief. They're bound to get the choker back.'

'It would be fun to go to Monte Carlo with ten thousand francs in our pockets.' Violet grinned. 'It *is* the casino capital of the world, after all.'

'Violet!' cried Garth. 'I thought you disapproved of gambling!'

'Only when it's just about luck. Playing a good game of cards is different. That's a skill.'

'All the more reason to let someone else get the reward. I don't want your father accusing me of leading you astray.'

'But it was *you* who *taught* me how to play poker!' protested Violet. She touched his arm. 'You're just jealous because now I win every time!'

Behind her an enormous carriage clock chimed six o'clock.

'Oh, no!' cried Violet.

'What's wrong?'

'We have to meet my parents in fifteen minutes!' Violet stood up. 'Do me a favour and tell them I'll be fashionably late.'

Garth opened his mouth to say that Lady Eleanor was *so* fashionably late that she always appeared at least half an hour after everyone else. But Violet was already running up the stairs, two steps at a time.

Twenty-five minutes later, Violet stood in front of the long mirror in her bedroom. She had chosen a simple evening dress of finely striped black and turquoise silk taffeta. The hem and sleeves were edged with a plaited ribbon of black satin and sewn with tiny silver stars. Her hair was drawn back as smoothly as she could manage and held up with two ebony combs. A single strand of gleaming jet beads lay around her neck.

She pulled on a bolero jacket in a heavier turquoise silk and checked herself in the mirror for the last time. She was not a beauty like her mother, but as she grew older she was beginning to learn that if she dressed simply she could make the best of her features, which were handsome rather than pretty. Her mother was famous for her high cheekbones, glossy blonde hair and green eyes. But Violet took after her father's side of the family. Her hair was dark and curly, and she had a long face with a wide mouth. Her eyes, however, were the startling blue of lapis lazuli.

'Such lovely eyes,' Lady Eleanor would murmur. 'From my Irish side of the family, of course.' And if Lord Percy was in the room, he would agree with his wife and raise his eyebrows at Violet.

Violet fixed a pair of turquoise stud earrings to her ears and gave the ebony combs a last push to hold them in place.

Then she picked up a silver evening purse and left her room, shutting the door behind her.

'Violet! You look quite the thing, you really do!' Lady Eleanor Winters held up her beautiful face for a kiss. As Violet bent down, her mother's perfume filled her nostrils. Lily-of-the-Valley — it was always the same.

'Percy,' cried Lady Eleanor as Violet straightened and looked around the room for Garth, 'I do believe Violet should have a glass of champagne tonight! We are in Paris, after all.'

Lord Percy smiled in agreement and turned to his

daughter. In Lord Percy's opinion, it was a blessing Violet was not a beauty like her mother and, for that matter, didn't share her mother's passion for clothes. Lord Percy knew that Violet wanted to go to university and he was sure that she had the determination to get what she wanted from life. He held out a glass of vintage champagne and raised his own towards her. 'You look lovely, my dear.'

'Thank you, Father,' said Violet. 'I am having the most exciting time already.' Violet sipped at her champagne and let the delicious bubbles fizz on her tongue. 'Have you seen Garth?'

'I presumed he spent the day with you and Madame,' replied Lord Percy.

For a moment, Violet was puzzled. It would only have taken Garth ten minutes to climb into his evening suit and stiff white collar. Why would he be so late?

But at that moment, Garth came into the room. A huge lady, dressed in a beaded gown with a spray of pink ostrich plumes attached to her elaborately piled hair, walked beside him. Her bosom was almost entirely covered with pearls and she wore an enormous square cut-diamond brooch on the neckline of her dress.

Violet almost cried out. It was Mrs Stuyvesant Fish from New York, one of the few of her mother's friends whom Violet actually liked. Garth must have met her in the hall. No wonder he had been late!

'Violet! My dear!' The great lady turned and beamed. 'How wonderful to see you! As I was telling Garth, you are both still the talk of the town in New York.' She reached out a hand whose every finger sparkled with rings and touched Violet on the cheek. 'Now, tell me, how is that little monkey of yours? I did think he was absolutely adorable.'

Mrs Stuyvesant Fish's fondness for Violet's pet monkey was one of the reasons Violet liked her so much. 'Homer's very well, thank you, but –' a shadow passed over Violet's face '– I'm afraid he has not come with me.'

'Why is that?' asked Mrs Stuyvesant Fish, frowning. 'A clever young monkey needs a change of scene. He would have *loved* Paris.' She paused. 'And now Garth tells me you are off to Monte Carlo. Just the place for Homer, I would have said.'

'I'm afraid my mother thought differently,' replied Violet. 'Especially since that time in New York when he took the Fabergé eggs and—'

'But he didn't *break* them!' interrupted Mrs Stuyvesant Fish. 'He was only curious. He *is* a monkey, after all.' She looked across the room to where Lady Eleanor sat, looking exquisite in a gown of sheer black silk, embroidered with seed pearls. 'But I know you understand these things better than your dear mother.'

Violet had a sudden vision of Homer shut up in his cage in the nursery of her parents' London house. Her throat went tight. 'There was no convincing my mother,' she murmured.

'Well, well. Then I shall introduce you to Toto.' Mrs Stuyvesant Fish patted Violet's arm. 'We all need fur in our lives, my dear.'

'Who's Toto?' asked Violet. As she spoke, Garth stepped forward. Against his dark suit, Violet hadn't noticed the black bundle nestled in the crook of his arm.

It was a miniature poodle puppy. Violet shrieked with delight as Garth passed the tiny dog into her arms.

'There you are, my dear,' said Mrs Stuyvesant Fish. 'And what's more, I have decided to come with you to Monte Carlo tomorrow.' She smiled into Violet's flushed, happy face. 'I shall need help looking after Toto.'

When Mrs Stuyvesant Fish had explained her new plan in detail, Lady Eleanor and Lord Percy were delighted. Their American friend had never been to Monte Carlo before, and it would give them a chance to pay her back for her kindness in New York.

Lady Eleanor patted Mrs Stuyvesant Fish lightly on the arm. 'Dear Gwendoline, I am imagining our days already! And, of course, you will join us for dinner tonight, won't you? We are dining with the Grand Duke Michael and his wife, Olga, and some friends of theirs who have just arrived in Paris this evening.' Lady Eleanor clapped her hands. 'It will be simply thrilling! You will be the envy of New York, I assure you.'

Mrs Stuyvesant Fish started to demur but at that moment two fabulously dressed women swept into the room. They were followed by two men, both in elegant tail coats and white ties. One of the men was tall with a full beard. The other had red hair that stuck up in tiny spikes from his head.

With her unerring social instinct, Lady Eleanor

turned just as the group was upon them and made the introductions.

It appeared that the man with red hair was Grand Duke Michael, and the shorter, squatter of the two women was his wife, Olga, who made up for her shape with an elaborate silver dinner gown. The tall man with the full beard was Count Drakensburg. Beside him, the Countess, whose hair was dark red, wore a necklace of emeralds over a low-cut fitted yellow dress trimmed with flounces of Belgian lace.

Once again, Lady Eleanor pressed Mrs Stuyvesant Fish to join their party, and this time she accepted, on the condition, she said smiling, that 'an old lady can be seated between the young ones'.

Two hours later, Violet watched as Countess Drakensburg sipped at a teaspoonful of sorbet flavoured with brandy. They were over halfway through dinner and everyone appeared to be enjoying themselves. Everyone, that is, except the Countess. Time and time again, Violet had seen her turn from the Grand Duke on her right to speak across the table to Mrs Stuyvesant Fish; but somehow there had never been a suitable pause in the conversation, and the Countess had had to give up.

Violet savoured the tangy sorbet. She remembered once listening with disbelief as Madame Poisson had explained how a sorbet was supposed to cut through the richness of an elaborate dinner – in this instance, salmon served with hollandaise sauce and roast goose stuffed with walnuts – to refresh the taste buds and restore the appetite for the courses still to come.

At the time Violet had thought it the strangest theory but now she knew that the right kind of sorbet did exactly what her governess had said.

Suddenly there was a lull in the conversation and Violet saw the Countess put down her spoon.

'I understand you are staying in Paris for the rest of the week, Mrs Stuyvesant Fish,' she said warmly. 'We would be delighted if you would join us at the opera tomorrow night.'

Mrs Stuyvesant Fish patted her mouth delicately with her damask napkin. 'How very kind of you, my dear Countess. And indeed, I would have so loved to come, but only this evening I decided to join Lord Percy and Lady Eleanor in Monte Carlo.' She smiled. 'It was a spur of the moment decision, you understand.'

Violet saw a strange expression flicker over the Countess's face. And as soon as it appeared, it went again. Violet looked down at the tablecloth so that she wouldn't be tempted to stare.

'But you *must* stay another night,' insisted the Countess. 'Why, it's the last performance of *La Bohème* and we have reserved a box!'

'Surely not especially for me, Countess?'

Violet looked up. There was a kind smile on Mrs Stuyvesant Fish's face, but her eyes looked puzzled.

The Countess smiled in return and added lightly that it was merely their custom to reserve a box for the final performance.

Immediately, the Count said something to Lord Percy and the two men laughed heartily. Then Garth asked Mrs Stuyvesant Fish about his New York friend Louis Cobolt, who had come to live in Paris.

'Gracious, what a silly old woman I am!' Mrs Stuyvesant Fish put down her sorbet spoon. 'I've been meaning to tell you his news all evening.'

It appeared that the odd exchange between the Countess and Mrs Stuyvesant was forgotten. Then Violet saw the now-familiar expression flicker across the Countess's face and suddenly she recognised it.

For some extraordinary reason, the Countess was annoyed.

Violet didn't understand. Could it be that Mrs Stuyvesant Fish had forgotten about the opera arrangement? But that was impossible. She and the Countess had not met before. Then again, perhaps Violet had missed something that had taken place earlier. She looked down the length of the table glittering with silverware and crystal, at her mother sitting at the end like a queen presiding over her court, her long diamond earrings flashing in the candlelight.

By the end of the dinner, Violet was tired. All the extraordinary things she had seen that day spun in her mind like so many pieces of coloured glass in a kaleidoscope. She stifled a yawn behind her hand.

At that moment, her mother rose. It was the signal for the ladies to withdraw and leave the gentlemen to their port and cigars. Violet stood up with Mrs Stuyvesant Fish.

'Will you excuse me?' she said in a low voice. 'I think I shall go to bed.'

'Exactly my intention, my dear,' replied Mrs Stuyvesant Fish. 'What with my new plans, I have many arrangements to make.'

Violet could feel eyes boring into her. She looked up just in time to see the Countess turn quickly away.

Violet felt a shiver of dislike. Once again she had a strong feeling that something was going on that she didn't understand. But she pushed it to the back of her mind. Tomorrow, they were going to Monte Carlo and she would never see the Count and Countess again.

THREE

Violet was dreaming she was doing handsprings with Marie Cherkassky along the seafront at Monte Carlo. She could feel the hard sand on the palms of her hands and the warm breeze whoosh under her full skirts as the two of them whirled over and over, laughing their heads off.

There was a gentle tap on her door, and she woke up, a big smile on her face. Bright sunlight was pouring in around the edges of the lacy curtains at her window. The tap came again.

'*Mademoiselle! Votre petit déjeuner, s'il vous plaît.*'

Violet sat up in bed and looked at her watch. It was nine o'clock! She had slept for almost ten hours!

What on earth would Garth say? They had arranged to meet in the front hall at half-past eight. Why hadn't someone woken her earlier?

'*Entrez! Entrez!*' Violet pulled on a fine lawn bed jacket and heaved herself up against the mountain of snowy pillows. She rubbed her eyes. She had never slept so deeply in all her life.

The door opened and a maid in a white cap and black uniform walked into the room, carrying a wide breakfast tray. She put it on one side of the bed and smoothed over the bed covers.

'*Bonjour, Mademoiselle!*'

'*Bonjour!*'

'*Quel beau temps!*'

'*Oui. Il fait beau.*'

Violet watched as the maid expertly poured out coffee and hot milk into a bowl, curtsied and left the room.

On her own again, Violet picked up the bowl and held it to her mouth with both hands. One of the things she loved best about France was drinking rich milky coffee from a bowl and not having to eat porridge for breakfast.

The tray was covered with a yellow linen cloth and

34

laid with porcelain hand-painted with wild flowers. A tiny bunch of violets sat in a vase in one corner.

It wasn't until Violet lifted up the napkin that covered the silver basket full of freshly baked *brioches* that she saw an envelope addressed to her in Garth's handwriting. *Urgent* was scrawled in the top left-hand corner.

Violet almost spilled her bowl of coffee as she ripped open the thick vellum paper.

Vi – bad news. Come to Mrs Stuyvesant Fish's suite asap. Garth

Violet heaved the tray to one side and jumped out of bed. As she pulled on her clothes, she asked herself again and again what could have happened. She felt a lump in her throat as she pushed her feet into her shoes. Mrs Stuyvesant Fish was not exactly what Garth would call a spring chicken. Was it possible she had fallen ill in the night?

Garth opened the door of Mrs Stuyvesant Fish's suite seconds after Violet knocked. She could see from his face that something dreadful had happened.

Her father was by the window, talking to the hotel manager in a low voice. Standing beside him was the *gendarme* whom Violet and Garth had seen the day before. Violet turned to Garth with her eyes wide. *What on earth was going on? And where was Mrs Stuyvesant Fish?*

Before Violet could speak, Garth led her into a small sitting room and shut the door.

Violet's heart hammered in her chest. 'Has she—' Violet began. Then she sat down and put her head in her hands. She couldn't bring herself to ask the question.

'She's not dead, Vi, if that's what you're thinking.' Garth sat down opposite her.

'Then what's *happened*?' Violet almost shouted. Her relief had turned into anger, and the only one to take it out on was Garth.

'Calm down, Vi. If we're going to help at all, we've got to think straight.' Garth paused and took a deep breath. 'Mrs Stuyvesant Fish's jewellery was stolen in the night. Apparently that big diamond brooch is priceless.'

Violet gasped. She knew the brooch was a family heirloom and that Mrs Stuyvesant Fish was particularly fond of it. 'Where is she now?'

'Resting,' replied Garth. 'Doctor's orders. When she discovered the theft, she collapsed.'

'How do you know all of this?'

'My rooms are next door,' said Garth. 'I got up early this morning to go for a walk. I was passing her door when she appeared in front of me, white as a sheet.' Garth shook his head. 'I thought she was going to have a heart attack. Anyway, I made her sit down, called the maid and the manager. Then I went to your parents' suite.'

'So that's why my father is here?'

Garth nodded. 'They've been trying to find the Duchamps to see if there are any similarities between the two robberies, but they must have gone out because their room is empty.'

At that moment, the door opened and Lord Percy walked into the little sitting room. His face was strained and tired. 'Good morning, my dear. It's a bad business, I'm afraid. Poor Gwendoline is taking it very hard.' He rubbed his hand over his forehead as if he was trying to clear his thoughts. 'She would like to see you in her bedroom.'

Violet jumped up but her father put a warning hand on her shoulder. 'Dr Jumeau is very worried about her, Violet. Try to stay calm.'

'Will she be able to come with us to Monte Carlo?'

'Absolutely not,' replied Lord Percy. 'She has a weak heart and Dr Jumeau has advised bed rest for at least two weeks.'

Violet followed her father across the main drawing room where the *gendarme* was still jotting in his note-book. The maid tapped on the bedroom door. A tall man in a black suit with a long face and a monocle appeared.

'Dr Jumeau, this is my daughter, Violet,' said Lord Percy.

The doctor smiled kindly. 'Come this way, my dear.'

Mrs Stuyvesant Fish was propped up in bed with her long white hair hanging loose around her shoulders. Her face seemed to have shrunk and there was something vulnerable and childlike about her. When she saw Violet, she patted the bed and Violet sat down beside her.

'I'm so sorry,' began Violet, almost in tears, then she remembered her father's warning, and tried to sound calm. 'If there is anything I can do to help, please tell me.'

Mrs Stuyvesant Fish squeezed Violet's hand. 'There

is something,' she said. 'That's why I asked for you. You see, it's all been a bit of a shock and now I can't look after him.' As she spoke, she lifted a corner of the peach satin coverlet and a fluffy black face appeared.

Violet patted her knees and Toto clambered towards her.

'Would you take care of him for me, my dear?' asked Mrs Stuyvesant Fish. 'He'd love the seaside in Monte Carlo and by the time you come back to Paris I shall be well enough to look after him again.'

'Of course I will!' cried Violet. 'In fact, I'd be absolutely delighted!' Then a thought suddenly occurred to her and she looked up anxiously. 'Only . . .'

'Don't worry,' said Mrs Stuyvesant Fish, reading Violet's mind. 'I've spoken to your father. He assures me your mother does not feel the same way about dogs as she does about monkeys.'

Toto stood up in Violet's lap and put his front paws on her chest. It was almost as if he wanted to be sure she had agreed to look after him.

'Good. That's settled.' Mrs Stuyvesant Fish leaned back on her pillows. 'Now all they have to do is find my diamond brooch.'

'I only wish Garth and I could help somehow,' said Violet.

'Don't you worry, my dear,' said Mrs Stuyvesant Fish. 'The *gendarme* assures me that they already have a number of suspects.' Her voice trailed away and she reached out and tickled Toto's ears. 'He loves his walks, don't you, Toto?'

Violet knew it was time to go and let Mrs Stuyvesant Fish rest. 'I'll take him out every day,' she promised. Then she turned and walked quickly out of the room.

'I wish there was something we could *do*,' said Garth as he and Violet walked over the cobbled square of the Place Vendôme. Toto pranced beside them at the end of his red lead, yapping excitedly at every dog he saw.

It was a beautiful spring morning and Violet could feel the warmth of the sun on her cheeks. She still couldn't believe her luck. For the first time ever, Madame Poisson had not insisted on accompanying her and Garth. Even though Violet knew her governess was visiting her uncle in Montparnasse to try and find a way of raising enough money to save the family farm in the Auvergne, her absence today was more than just the urgency of a family problem. It seemed to Violet that in her dear codfish's mind, there was something about walking a dog that made it permissible for her to go out on her own with Garth as her chaperon. Whatever the reason, Violet found the sense of freedom exhilarating.

'What are you looking so happy about?' asked Garth. 'Do you know something I don't?'

Violet laughed and pulled Toto back to stop him from wrapping his lead around her ankles. 'I was trying to understand the relationship between a poodle and freedom of movement,' she replied. 'Unaccountably, I've got both!'

'So how about using your new-found freedom to apply your mind to these jewel robberies?'

'Mrs Stuyvesant Fish said the police already had a few suspects,' said Violet. 'I couldn't exactly ask her whether they were known criminals or members of the hotel staff.'

'Pity those people haven't shown up.'

'You mean the Duchamps?'

'Yeah. I asked a valet if they had checked out and he said they hadn't.' Garth paused. 'The *gendarmes* have been hanging around waiting for them since breakfast.'

'Maybe they went out for a walk to clear their heads – she did look very shaken last night.' Violet paused. 'By the way, have they found out how the robberies were carried out?'

Garth nodded. 'It's pretty straightforward if you know about safes. There's one in every suite. The *gendarmes* are sure the thieves got in in the middle of the night and cracked the combination locks.'

'They must have been very quiet,' replied Violet.

'Professional safe-breakers usually are,' said Garth.

On the far side of the square, they saw a shiny purple hansom cab stop in front of the hotel. A tall woman, dressed in an emerald-green day dress with an elaborate black ruffle around the collar, stepped onto the street. A man with a beard, wearing a top hat, stepped down after her. It was Count and Countess Drakensburg.

Suddenly Violet remembered the Countess's insistence that Mrs Stuyvesant Fish join them at the opera that night and the look of annoyance that had passed over her face when her invitation was turned down. She told Garth and he shrugged. He said he'd found the Count smug and pushy. So, when dinner had finished and the ladies had left the room, after one small glass of port, Garth had made his excuses to Lord Percy and left to read the latest Sherlock Holmes mystery in his room.

'There was something pushy about *her*, too,' said Violet. 'I hope they don't force themselves on Mrs Stuyvesant Fish.'

'They won't. Dr Jumeau has given out strict instructions that she is not to be disturbed.' Garth shrugged. 'They've probably just come to leave a note or something to say how sorry they are about the theft.'

Violet stared as she watched the doorman in his purple and gold uniform open the door. 'How would they know about it?'

'Bad news travels fast.' Garth suddenly sat down on a bench. 'It's hopeless, Vi. There's nothing we can do to help. There's no time.' He threw a stick for Toto to chase. 'Let's talk about something else. Tell me about this fancy train we're taking tonight. I heard an American talking about it in the lobby today.'

Violet sat down beside him. 'The good news is that

43

it's all blue and gold and goes really fast. The bad news is that everyone has to dress for dinner.'

Violet knew that one of the things Garth liked least about English society was the formal dressing up – especially having to wear tail coats in the evening. He hated the stiff white shirt fronts and collars and the stiff manners that went with them.

'I don't believe it.' Garth groaned. 'What about Monte Carlo? Is it formal there, too? I thought maybe being in the south by the sea . . .' His voice trailed away.

'It's *always* formal in the evening, Garth.' Violet nudged his elbow. 'You know that. But we'll be able to get away on our own during the day. And Monte Carlo is full of eccentrics. Look at Marie.'

Garth groaned again. He had managed to push the memory of the crazy Russian from his mind. Now her incessant jabbering came back to him. 'That lunatic better not follow us around everywhere.'

'Don't be so ungentlemanly,' laughed Violet. 'For all you know, she might be part of some strange mystery.'

'That'll be the day,' said Garth. 'Anyway, I think our chance for solving mysteries was here in Paris and we've missed it.' He picked up another stick and threw it as far as he could. 'Fetch, Toto!' he commanded.

The little dog rolled over on his back and looked at him sideways.

Garth felt a flush of annoyance creep up his neck. The day had started badly and now it was getting worse.

'Cheer up, cross-patch,' said Violet. 'Maybe you'll meet someone strange and exciting on the way to Monte Carlo.'

'How much do you want to bet?'

Violet stood up. 'A hundred francs?'

'Done!'

Madame Poisson stared out of the hansom cab as they made their way around the Place de la République towards the Gare du Nord. Beside her, Garth and Violet were playing a silly game of 'I Spy' in French and, while normally the governess would have joined in to widen their vocabulary beyond 'horse', 'wheel', 'hat' and 'umbrella', at that moment all she could think about was her visit to Montparnasse and her uncle's terrible words.

The farm will have to be sold, Amélie. The bank has demanded their loan is paid back by Easter. Your mother and brother have no money to pay it.

Madame Poisson felt her head go dizzy and cold. Les Pradelles had been her childhood home. It was where she had learned to cook and sew and where she had been taught by Sister Hortense from the local convent, who'd recognised her shy intelligence and helped her with the examinations to get into university. The thought that Les Pradelles had to be sold was unbearable.

But Uncle Hugo was adamant. It would take a miracle or a pot of gold to save the situation.

Madame Poisson looked out of the window and found herself staring at a grassy bank planted with daffodils in the shape of a clover leaf.

'The ace of spades,' cried Garth, also looking out of the window, trying to guess what Violet was looking at, 'or whatever that is in French.'

'Wrong!' said Violet. 'It's a clover!' She turned. 'Isn't it, Madame?'

But Madame Poisson didn't reply. A week ago, before she knew about the farm, she would never have allowed the thought that had suddenly appeared in her mind to take root. Now, the little governess let her mind travel to her own bank account and count up the small amount of savings she had managed to set aside.

The gambling rooms of Monte Carlo were not unfamiliar to her. Two years ago, when she had first become Violet's governess and joined the family on their visit to the South of France, she had occasionally visited the casino herself during her time off. Indeed, her winnings at the card table had contributed to her savings. Because, apart from possessing a fine intelligence, Madame Poisson was a brilliant poker player.

As the hansom cab rattled under the great vaulted roof of the bustling train station, a plan to save Les Pradelles was rapidly taking shape in Madame Poisson's mind.

FOUR

It was sheer luck that Violet happened to be looking out of her compartment window when the porter went past, pushing an enormous trolley stacked with luggage. As she stared at all the different-shaped boxes and cases, Violet wondered how on earth *anyone* could possibly need so much luggage for one season at Monte Carlo. It was almost three times what her mother took with her, and Lady Eleanor was famously extravagant.

A man jumped down from a cab and spoke quickly to the porter, waving him in the direction of the first-class carriages. Violet's jaw dropped open. It was Henri Duchamps!

Violet remembered her bet with Garth and almost shouted with delight.

Could it be that the Duchamps' jewels had been recovered and they had decided to go south for a holiday? At any rate, they would almost certainly know something about Mrs Stuyvesant Fish's missing diamond brooch.

A wide grin spread across Violet's face. Garth owed her a hundred francs!

An hour later, Violet made her way down the swaying corridor of the train to the saloon carriage. At the far end she could see her mother sitting in one of the blue plush armchairs in deep conversation with the woman she now knew was Florence Duchamps. The two could not have looked more different. Florence Duchamps' severe black silk dress was softened only by a simple necklace of rubies and a black ostrich-feather boa. Opposite her, Lady Eleanor wore a maroon organza gown with a flounced, tiered skirt, which fell to the floor like a waterfall. Around her neck was a five-string choker of pearls fastened to a large oval diamond surrounded by amethysts. As usual, Lady Eleanor wore very little make-up, while Florence Duchamps had the same scarlet slash of lipstick that Violet remembered from the boulevard the day before.

Lady Eleanor looked up as Violet came into the carriage. 'Darling, may I introduce you to Madame Duchamps? You will, of course, have heard of her terrible loss at the hotel.'

Violet took the small cold hand that was offered. It was like holding a dead fish. 'I am delighted to meet you,' she said. She waited to see if the woman would recognise her but, despite a flicker in her cold eyes, she appeared not to. 'Is there any news from the *gendarmes*?'

'Sadly not,' replied Florence Duchamps, 'despite the offer of a reward. I was telling your mother that we are considering employing the services of a private detective. The choker belonged to my mother and it was very precious to me.'

'Will the detective act for Mrs Stuyvesant Fish as well?' asked Violet.

'I cannot say,' replied Florence Duchamps. 'We left the hotel shortly after the theft of my choker.'

'You mean you never spoke to the *gendarmes* who were investigating Mrs Stuvesant Fish's theft?' blurted out Violet.

A faint flush passed over Florence Duchamps' face.

'Really, Violet,' said Lady Eleanor. 'You mustn't tire Madame Duchamps with your questions. She has been up since dawn making new arrangements. Why, they almost missed the train!'

Violet tried not to stare at Madame Duchamps. If they had been up since dawn, how could they not have known that the detective working for Mrs Stuyvesant Fish wanted urgently to speak to them? Not only that, Violet was sure Madame Duchamps *had* recognised her.

But Violet also knew that in her mother's mind missing a train was almost as bad as breaking a leg and that Lady Eleanor was in full flow, extending sympathy and understanding. If Violet asked any more questions, she would blot her copybook for the rest of the journey.

Violet made her excuses and looked around for Garth. He wasn't there but she recognised a tall American couple from the Ritz. At the far end of the carriage, her father was talking to Henri Duchamps. Before he saw her and insisted on an introduction, Violet sat down in a plush swivel armchair and turned it towards the window.

On the other side of the glass, the countryside was turning gold in the setting sun. In the middle of a patchwork of fields, Violet could see a church steeple towering over a cluster of houses. A farmer in a hat and dark blue workman's smock sat on his cart on a dusty track and waited for the great blue and gold train to clatter past. For a split second Violet felt he was looking straight at her and it occurred to her that he had probably never even been to Paris. Yet she, at fourteen, had already travelled halfway around the world.

'Penny for your thoughts, Lady Vi.' Garth swung into the seat opposite her and, before she had a chance to reply, he said, 'I'd bet good money that Henri Duchamps saw me on the boulevard, yet just now when your father introduced him he pretended he'd never seen me before.'

Violet looked into Garth's face. 'His wife did the same to me. And do you know, they never even talked to the *gendarme* who was helping Mrs Stuyvesant Fish!'

'Huh.' Garth looked quickly over his shoulder. 'Your parents seem rather taken by them.'

Violet followed his glance and, in that moment,

she decided she didn't like the Duchamps. Henri Duchamps' face was sharp and arrogant. As she looked at him, she thought of Florence's cold, slimy handshake and shivered.

'Sometimes, my parents have the strangest taste in people,' said Violet. 'I only hope my mother doesn't take them on as her new best friends.'

There was a yapping noise. A flustered maid appeared at Violet's side with Toto squirming in her arms.

'Excuse me, Mademoiselle, but I making your bed, he run away!' explained the maid in an embarrassed, breathless voice. '*Mauvais chien!* He eat his cage!' As she spoke, Toto squirmed one last time and jumped from her arms. Then, before anyone had a chance to grab him, he was running down the carriage, barking.

By the time Violet caught up with him, he was panting beside her mother's chair.

Lady Eleanor looked up and the smile on her beautiful face curdled. 'Violet,' she said in a dangerously smooth voice, 'remove this creature immediately.'

'Yes, Mother. I'm so sorry. He chewed through his cage.'

'How he came to be here is of no interest to me.' Lady Eleanor turned back to Florence Duchamps. 'I do apologise, Florence.'

Florence Duchamps gave Violet a friendly smile. 'Please, my dear. Don't worry on my account.' Then her smile froze as Toto squeezed through the forest of legs, stopped in front of her husband and began to snarl.

A moment later, there was a yelp of pain as Toto sank his tiny sharp teeth into Henri Duchamps's ankle.

'Curse the little rat!' Henri Duchamps shook his trouser leg furiously but nothing would dislodge the snarling puppy.

'Toto!' cried Violet, her cheeks crimson. She had never seen a puppy take such an instant dislike to anyone. She bent down to grab him but once again Toto was too quick for her. He let go of the trouser leg and scrambled under a chair, barking as loudly as he could.

'I'm very sorry, Monsieur Duchamps,' cried Violet. Her face was bright red and her black curly hair hung in straggles.

Lord Percy smiled benignly at his only daughter. 'Henri, may I introduce my daughter, Violet?'

Violet shook the fine-boned hand that was offered to her. It was like holding a bundle of dry sticks. 'I'm sorry,' she said again. 'I don't know what's got into him.'

'Please don't concern yourself.' Henri Duchamps tried to smile, but his grey eyes were stony in his smooth-shaven face. 'Perhaps the train has unnerved him.'

'Yes, I'm sure you're right.' Violet bent down to make another grab for Toto as Garth appeared at her side.

'Allow me.' Garth opened his hand to reveal a tiny round of toast spread with *foie gras*. 'I'm told the canapés are irresistible.'

A moment later, Violet held Toto securely in her arms.

'Nicely done, young man!' said Lord Percy, resolutely ignoring the steely looks coming from the direction of his wife. It suddenly occurred to Violet that perhaps her father had only been pretending to like Henri Duchamps. At any rate, he seemed to be hugely enjoying his discomfort.

Then Violet caught her mother's eye and left the carriage as quickly as she could.

*

Madame Poisson was waiting for Violet in her own compartment. The maid would have reported every detail of the incident and Violet braced herself for a torrent of blame. Instead, the little French woman only shook her head and pointed to a wooden box with a handle and a wire mesh door at one end.

'*Ma pauvre!* cried Madame Poisson. 'How upsetting for you, and, I am quite sure, for your mother also.' She bent down and opened the mesh door. 'Mrs Stuyvesant Fish sent this on. The porter has only just delivered it to me.'

Without waiting for a reply, Madame Poisson picked up Toto. As she did so, Violet noticed a pack of cards lying open at her table. Beside it was a notebook and four tidy lists of numbers.

'Have you been playing patience, Madame?' asked Violet. She knew from Garth that her governess was a brilliant card player but for some reason she had never played with Violet. Perhaps it was Madame who had taught Garth to play poker. At any rate, it occurred to Violet that it would be fun to play a hand with her dear codfish and perhaps it might take her mind off her worries about Les Pradelles. Ever since Violet was little, Madame Poisson had told her stories of her life as a young girl on the farm and Violet knew that the possibility of losing it had upset her desperately.

She picked up a card and turned it over. It was the ace of spades. 'Garth has taught me to play cards, Madame,' she said, almost hesitantly, as if she was worried that her governess would be cross. 'He says I'm better than him now but that you are very good.'

Violet looked into Madame's round, pop-eyed face. There were shadows under her eyes and lines on her forehead. She looked as if she hadn't slept properly since they'd arrived in Paris.

'Would you play cards with me?' asked Violet kindly. She smiled to make her governess smile. 'We are going to Monte Carlo, after all!'

Madame Poisson took the ace of spades from Violet's hand and put it back on the pile. 'Perhaps one day we will, Violette,' she said in a faraway voice. 'But now you must make peace with Lady Eleanor.'

'Yes,' said Violet simply. 'What do you suggest I say to her?'

'First tidy your hair,' replied Madame Poisson. She closed the notebook with the lines of figures as if somehow she wanted to hide them. Then she looked into Violet's deep blue eyes and smiled. 'If I were you, I'd make no mention of Toto at all. As to a topic of conversation, I understand everyone is talking about the Russian Ballet.'

Madame Poisson reached out and tucked a strand of Violet's dark curly hair back into place. 'We'll be in Monte Carlo tomorrow. She will have forgotten all about Toto by then.'

'Allow me, Lady Violet!' said a deep American voice. Violet stepped quickly aside as a broad-shouldered man with a square jaw and slicked-back hair reached over her head and held open the connecting door to the saloon carriage. She recognised him from the lobby at the Ritz.

Violet looked into the man's broad, friendly face and walked into the carriage. 'Thank you!'

'Frank C. Winalot!' The man held out his hand. 'I don't believe we've met but I've just been talking to Garth. In fact, I've offered him a ride on my yacht!' He grinned. 'It's a brand-new one that's just been launched in Monte Carlo.'

'You could come too, if you want!' A tiny young woman with a wide smile and bright brown eyes appeared from behind Frank Winalot's other arm. She held out her hand. 'I'm Lily. Frank's wife.'

The tall American laughed. 'How can I make fancy introductions if you always beat me to it, honey?'

The openness of the two Americans delighted Violet, even though she knew that in her mother's world if a person's connections were not the right sort they were unacceptable. For some reason this applied particularly to foreigners. And especially to Americans.

Violet heard her mother's voice in her head: *The ones who force their way into good society in Europe are most likely shut out from it in their own country.* Lady Eleanor had assured her daughter that an American — *of the right sort, of course* — had made this observation. But then how could her mother be so sure of someone like Florence Duchamps? Violet wondered. She knew nothing of *her* connections and surely it was not enough simply to be a fellow guest at the Ritz.

At that moment, Lady Eleanor appeared at Violet's side. 'Violet, my dear. I would like you to meet Monsieur Duchamps. He's a great admirer of Descartes.'

Violet felt her face prickle with embarrassment.

Her mother had not even deigned to acknowledge the Winalots, standing beside her. It was her way of telling Violet that the Winalots were not the right sort.

How could she be so *rude*?

'I have already met Monsieur Duchamps, Mother,' replied Violet, trying to keep her voice even and ignoring her dear codfish's advice. 'Toto bit his ankle, if you recall.' Violet turned. 'May I introduce Mr and Mrs Winalot? They have very kindly invited Garth and me to go sailing on their yacht while we are staying in Monte Carlo.'

Frank and Lily shook Lady Eleanor's hand. 'We'd be honoured if you would come, too,' said Frank. 'The yacht's a real beauty.' He smiled down at his tiny wife. 'I've called her *Lily*.'

'How *enchanting*,' replied Lady Eleanor in an off-hand voice. 'What a *charming* invitation.'

Frank smiled. 'My pleasure. I like meeting people and I've never been to Monte Carlo before.' He paused. 'I understand you know it well.'

Lady Eleanor raised her eyebrows. 'Do you indeed?'

Frank smiled again. 'Mrs Stuyvesant Fish is a close

friend of my mother. She speaks highly of you and your family.'

Violet could have whooped with delight. But before her mother had time to collect herself and reply properly, a waiter appeared and announced dinner.

'Violet, darling,' said Lady Eleanor quietly. A vague look of discomfort passed over her delicate features. 'The Duchamps have asked us to join them for dinner. Would you mind dreadfully? I, ah, have arranged for you and Garth to sit at your own table.'

Which is why you haven't mentioned Toto, thought Violet. She knew her mother kept an extremely accurate mental record of offences committed and offences forgiven. By standing up her own daughter for dinner, she could convince herself they were now even.

'We would be delighted if Garth and Violet would dine with us,' cried Lily. She turned to Violet. 'That is, if—'

'We would *love* to,' said Violet quickly.

The dining car had tables of four down one side and two down the other. Each one was covered with a white damask cloth and glittered with crystal glasses and silver candlesticks. Finely pleated lace blinds had been pulled down over the windows. It was like the Ritz in miniature.

Violet sat beside Frank Winalot, opposite Lily and Garth, and stared at the menu. It seemed extraordinary that the chef on board could produce a ten-course meal from a kitchen that was barely larger than her own sleeping compartment. There were oysters, then turtle soup, followed by dishes of langoustine, salmon, guinea fowl and baby chicken. Violet let her eyes wander over the French words – *chaud-froid de langoustes, bécasses à la Parisienne.*

'What does *bécasses* mean?' Violet asked.

'Search me,' said Frank. 'It sure ain't a steak sandwich, that's all I know.'

'Honestly, Frank,' said Lily as she picked up her napkin. 'You really must learn to eat what's put in front of you.'

'It means woodcock,' translated Garth. 'They're little game birds. I don't like them.'

'I'd say that makes four of us,' said Frank. He nodded to a waiter, who filled their glasses with champagne from a bottle in a silver bucket on a stand.

Then he raised his glass. 'To luck at the gambling table and adventure on the high seas!'

As Violet raised her own glass, she suddenly saw Florence Duchamps staring thoughtfully at Garth. She knew then, without a doubt, that the French woman had seen them both on the boulevard.

As the icy bubbles slithered down her throat for the second time in two days, Violet felt a cold fizzy excitement creep over her.

It was the same feeling she always had when there was a mystery in the air!

FIVE

When Violet woke up the next morning, the train was winding along the ridge of a steep limestone cliff. She pulled back the lacy curtains of her compartment window. It was as if a picture postcard had come to life.

Far below, the turquoise Mediterranean Sea sparkled in the peach-pink light of the rising sun. Brightly coloured fishing boats with white and tan sails were anchored far out on the glittering water. Tall feathery palm trees grew along the shore, sheltering cottages painted lilac, pink and terracotta. Yellow mimosa bushes appeared to grow wild, and every gate and fence was crawling with green bougainvillea leaves, dotted with deep purple flowers.

Violet pulled open the ventilation grille as far as it would go. Even with the speed of the train, she could feel the warmth in the air. She pushed back her linen sheets and swung out of her bunk bed to wash her face in the porcelain basin on the other side of the compartment. Her maid had hung up a fine lawn skirt printed with mint-green polka dots, a finely pleated white blouse and a scarlet linen jacket. Violet pulled on light cotton underclothes and dressed herself in five minutes. It took another two minutes to drag a brush through her curly hair and tie it back with a red ribbon.

At that moment, the train blew its whistle twice and began to slow down. Violet ran down the corridor and into the breakfast carriage. It was empty except for Garth, who was staring out of the window, chewing a *croissant*.

'We'll be in Nice in ten minutes,' he said, as Violet sat down opposite him. His eyes were bright and Violet felt the same excitement building up inside her. She had been dreaming of their arrival for weeks now.

'We'll have time to walk along the promenade,'

said Violet, grinning. 'It always takes hours to get the luggage unloaded and sent on to Monte Carlo. It has to go by wagon.'

A waiter poured strong black coffee into a china bowl and filled it up with hot milk. More *croissants* were put on the table.

'Sounds terrific to me,' replied Garth. He reached across and grabbed a *croissant*. 'I can't get enough of these things!' He dunked the pastry in his bowl of coffee and bit into it.

'Yuck,' said Violet, watching him. 'I don't know how you can eat it all soggy like that.'

'It's not *soggy*,' said Garth. He looked at her. 'Besides, it's how *real* French people eat them.'

Violet ignored him and spread her own *croissant* with homemade apricot jam.

'So, what's this promenade?' asked Garth.

'It's called the Promenade des Anglais,' explained Violet. 'It was built so the English could walk beside the sea and gossip about each other.'

'And where are we staying in Monte Carlo?' Garth took another *croissant*.

'The Hermitathe,' said Violet, with her mouth full. She laughed and put her hand up to stop herself spraying bits of *croissant* all over the table. At the other end of the carriage a waiter watched them disdainfully.

'What will your parents do while we're exploring Nice?' asked Garth.

'They'll wait at the Hôtel des Anglais while the porters make the arrangements.' Violet took another *croissant*. 'The problem is the codfish.'

'I thought you had a furry passport to freedom,' said Garth as he finished his coffee.

'Of course! Toto! We'll take him for a walk.' Then Violet's face darkened. 'Poor Madame, I can tell she's awfully worried that her family are going to lose their farm. Do you think I should mention it to my father? I know he'd find a way to help.'

Garth put down his cup. 'I'm sure he'll lend her the money.'

'Madame would never accept a loan,' replied Violet firmly. 'She's too proud.'

Garth swallowed the last of his *croissant*. 'Then I'd leave that to him. He'll find a way.'

At that moment, the train blew its whistle and pulled into the station.

*

Half an hour later Violet was breathing in the sweet, rich smell of orange blossom as she walked out of the Hôtel des Anglais with Toto tugging at his lead. In front of her, the Promenade des Anglais was already bustling with people. Beyond, Garth was skimming stones into the surf.

Inside the hotel, in the rose-and-green morning room, Lady Eleanor was recovering from the train trip and reading the *Monte Carlo Gazette* to find out who had arrived and what calls she should make. In another room Lord Percy was busy giving instructions to the porters to send the luggage to their suite at the Hermitage. Once it was on its way, and Lady Eleanor felt able, they would travel the last part of the journey in a horse-drawn cab. It was just as Violet had described to Garth. Her parents' routine never changed.

Violet had expected the Duchamps to be staying at the same hotel as them in Monte Carlo, but it turned out that they were staying at the Riviera Palace, which was half a mile away. Garth had been disappointed at the news. If there was something suspicious going on, it would have been much easier to spy on them if they were under the same roof. But Violet had been pleased. Perhaps now her mother would involve herself with her usual group of aristocratic friends. Of course, some of *them* were pompous and boring, but at least they weren't pretending to be anything else. Violet had the overriding feeling that there was something calculating about the Duchamps – as if they were trying too hard to be accepted in the right circles.

Now, as she stood and watched men in straw boater hats and women carrying lacy parasols stroll along the promenade, Violet suddenly remembered that Madame Poisson had particularly asked her to take a parasol with her and she had forgotten. Earlier that morning, Toto had worked his magic and the little Frenchwoman hadn't questioned the fact that Garth and Violet would be on their own. Indeed, she had seemed just as distracted as she had been on the train, and when Violet had found her in a quiet corner of the hotel, once again there was a pack of cards open on the table in front of her and a notebook with yet more lists of cards and numbers. This time, Violet made no mention of playing cards together for fun. Madame's face was altogether too serious.

Even so, Violet didn't want to risk Madame seeing

her from the hotel window without a parasol and calling her back. She quickly crossed the road and called down to Garth, who was still skimming stones. If they set off now, there would be time to explore the flower market before her parents left for the Hermitage.

'Lady Violet! A thousand welcomes!'

Violet spun around and found herself looking into Marie Cherkassky's beaming face. She was dressed in a flowing black and orange kimono under a long green tunic, and wore scarlet boots on her feet.

Before Violet had time to hold out her hand, Marie had wrapped her arms around Violet's neck and kissed her firmly on both cheeks. 'Yes! Yes!' she cried. 'My friends are here at last! I am happy, happy, happy!'

Garth, who had seen Marie rush along the promenade towards Violet, now joined them, but stood a little way apart. The idea of being slobbered on by a crazy Russian made him feel sick. 'I hope you are well, Miss Cherkassky,' he said, refusing to budge from behind the safety of a palm tree.

Marie stared at him, her eyes blazing. 'I am maddened with joy at the sight of you!' she shrieked.

A moment later, despite Garth's best efforts, Marie

managed to manoeuvre herself between them and link arms. 'My friends,' she shrieked again. Then she swept them down the promenade, with Toto leading the way and leaping about like a jack-in-the-box.

By the time they had walked for half an hour, Marie had called out greetings to every other passer-by whether, it soon became clear to Violet, she knew them or not. But not even a complete stranger could resist smiling back or, in the case of one man, raising his boater and making a short bow.

'Of course, when I speak to the people like this,' Marie explained in a serious voice, 'you must remember I am speaking to my audience. Or rather, what *will* be my audience.'

Violet frowned. 'What audience?'

'My audience for when I am the famous concert pianist.' Marie stopped and waved her arms in the air. 'They will remember seeing the great Cherkassky walking with her English friends in Monte Carlo. Also today, a grand piano comes by cart to my mother's apartment and soon she will be looking for subscriptions, so it is good I make the impressions this moment so these people will remember me and give lots of money.'

Violet had no idea what Marie was talking about. Surely Marie's mother didn't approach complete strangers to ask for money to support her daughter's musical career? Violet was about to ask, when she suddenly remembered Marie's governess. Where was she?

'Ah, the porpoise – Tanenko,' said Marie when Violet enquired. 'I gave her the petticoat, as you Americans say.'

Garth stared at her and Violet burst out laughing. 'You mean *the slip*, Marie,' said Violet. 'That's what we say. You gave her the slip.'

'Any kind of undergarment,' agreed Marie impatiently.

'Yes, I leave her in the Grand Hotel tea-rooms, take the fresh air and go through the hedgerow backwards.' She flung out her arms, obviously delighted with her own cleverness. 'She never follow me here.'

Violet was just about to ask where Marie was staying when the Russian slapped her own forehead. 'But of course, you come now to see my piano. It is worth my mother's diamonds, I assure you.'

For a moment, Violet wondered if Marie had mixed up her words again. 'You mean your mother has sold her jewellery to buy you a piano?'

Marie shrugged. 'Of course. I am a genius.' She laughed at their serious faces. 'She also buys time while my father looks for his pen to write a cheque. It is the way with many Russians.'

Still Violet didn't understand. She thought of Countess Drakensburg, dripping with diamonds. 'But I heard Russians had lots of money and even more jewellery,' she said.

Marie cocked her head playfully, as if the conversation was turning into a riddle. 'No, no, my dear Violet. Well, some perhaps. Not most. No cash and paste jewellery. Cash is difficult to fake, of course. But no one knows what is paste and what is real unless they carry a magnifying glass on a string around their wrist.'

Violet could tell that Garth was as intrigued as she was. She pointed to a bench ahead of them. 'Would you tell us about these paste diamonds, Marie?'

Marie clapped her hands, hurried over to the bench, sat down and arranged her skirts. 'Come! Come!' she cried. 'I give you my best lesson!'

For the next hour Marie told Garth and Violet everything she knew about fake diamonds. They learned how the paste diamonds were made of powdered glass and crafted by the finest jewellers in Paris and how many women wore them now instead of real diamonds. At this point, Marie's eyes went wide. 'And sometimes ladies wear them to pretend they are real diamonds, to make right friends if you understand me.

'And also,' continued Marie, 'you should know another reason, that is thieves are stealing diamonds, so many ladies now wear fakes ones.' She chuckled and patted Violet's hand. 'Of course the thiefs know the difference but they are difficult to catch, these bad thiefs, because they are not dressing bad. Many times, they are looking the same as real rich people. Especially here, in Monte Carlo.' Marie shrugged her shoulders up to her ears. 'My mother say, who knows what is gentlemens and what is thiefs?'

Marie threw back her head and laughed. 'As you see, my mother speak terrible English.'

Garth rubbed his hands over his face. 'And you think these thieves may be in Monte Carlo?'

'Indeed yes,' replied Marie. 'Every season same. Always bad, bad people around gambling wheels.' She smiled at them. 'So Russians maybe not so silly to wear paste.'

Violet said nothing for a moment. She was trying to imagine telling her mother all this. In her mind's eye, she could see Lady Eleanor's exquisite eyebrows lift a fraction. *Really, Violet, you've been reading too many adventure stories.*

At that moment, there were two sharp blasts on what sounded like a policeman's whistle. Marie jumped up from the bench and stared wildly down the promenade.

'*Nyet!*' she cried. 'No!' Madame Tanenko was bearing down on them with the speed of a porpoise riding a torpedo.

'*A bientôt, mes amis!*' Marie gathered up her skirts and ran swiftly across the main street. 'What is your hotel?' she shouted over her shoulder.

'The Hermitage!' replied Violet.

'*Gardez bien vos diamants!*

Violet and Garth watched as Marie disappeared into a tangle of alleyways. Further up the street, Madame Tanenko ducked down another alley and set off after her, furiously blowing her whistle.

'She'll cut her off at the pass,' said Garth in his best cowboy accent. But inside he was thinking about what Marie had just told them.

'Good thing we're staying at the smartest place in town,' he said after a while, when they gave up watching the chase.

'Why?'

'Sounds like it's where to look for diamond thieves.'

'Maybe the same gang from the Ritz will try their luck down here.' Violet stood up and dusted the sand from her skirt. 'Wouldn't it be great to find Mrs Stuyvesant Fish's brooch?'

Garth looked at her. 'Maybe we should take tea at the Riviera Palace and get to know the Duchamps.'

Violet shuddered. 'Why? They're not thieves. I mean, they wouldn't steal their own diamonds, would they?' She looked around and whistled for Toto, who was barking at the waves.

'Who knows?' replied Garth. 'Anyway, there's something peculiar about them.' He bent down and patted Toto's back as Violet clipped on his lead. 'Come on. Let's go and find your parents. I could kill for a *pain au chocolat*.'

SIX

Violet stood in her bedroom at the Hermitage. On the floor by her door was a small wicker basket done up with leather straps. An envelope was sitting on top, addressed in her mother's elegant copperplate hand. Violet glared at the basket then turned and stared angrily out of the window. It was the same view she'd seen from the train. The sea was still there. So were the fishing boats, the palm trees and the gaily-painted cottages, but this morning everything looked dull and flat and boring. Violet stamped her foot, unable to contain her fury a minute longer. It was so unfair! Ever since they had arrived at the Hermitage, Violet had been dragged around Monte

Carlo to meet boring old ladies and make conversation with their dull-witted daughters, while Garth had been allowed to wander about the town on his own and get to know the maze of little streets, strange shops and pretty squares. Yesterday, while Violet had to sit through tea with a distant German cousin of King Edward, Garth had hitched a lift on the back of a flower-grower's cart and spent the day in the mountains. And today, just when Violet was expecting some free time so the two of them could visit the Riviera Palace and spy on the Duchamps, Garth and her father had been invited pigeon-shooting and Violet had been ordered by her mother to deliver a basket of smoked fish to some crusty aristocratic lady her father had once known.

'Really, dear, Caroline Egmont is very much looking forward to your visit,' Lady Eleanor had said in an exasperated voice that morning. 'If you are going to be sulky, we will have to send you and Madame Poisson back to London.'

Now, as Violet looked out of her window, she saw a donkey pulling a cart loaded with wine barrels clip-clop past a bright blue Rolls-Royce. The cart stopped in front of the hotel and Violet watched as her mother got out. She was dressed entirely in lilac and carrying a yellow silk parasol.

Violet stuck her tongue out at her. With an eerie sixth sense, Lady Eleanor looked up and waved cheerily. Luckily, she was too far away to see the expression on her daughter's face. She handed over two beautifully wrapped parcels to the doorman and slipped back into the gloom of the huge car. It was Lady Eleanor's custom to spend the mornings shopping before she changed her clothes for her luncheon appointment; and there was still time for at least two more shopping expeditions before changing for dinner.

Violet scooped up the wicker basket from the floor, stuffed the envelope inside and stomped out of the room. The sooner she got away from the Hermitage the better. She was just about to run down the stairs into the hall, when Countess Drakensburg walked purposefully through the front door.

For a split second, Violet froze. The shock of seeing the Countess changed her mood completely. The last thing she wanted was to speak to the woman. Just in time, Violet managed to duck behind a big spray of mimosa blossoms by the banisters on the first landing.

From where she was hiding she could see the top of the Countess's elegant straw hat and the gleam of her dark red hair. But what on earth was she doing in Monte Carlo? Only two nights ago, she had been so definite about staying in Paris. Then she heard the Countess's high, brittle voice talking to the manager and Violet felt the hairs prickle on the back of her neck.

'The Lavender Suite? Excellent! We will be near our good friends, Lord and Lady Winters.'

Violet gasped out loud. What on earth was the Countess talking about? She had only met her parents once!

Violet peered out from behind the mimosa just in time to see Countess Drakensburg disappear through a pair of double doors into the main drawing room.

Then she walked quickly to the front hall, where the head porter was organising the newly arrived luggage to be taken to the Drakensburgs' suite.

There was a veritable mountain of cases and trunks and hatboxes. It looked as if the Count and Countess were going to move into the Hermitage for the rest of the year.

Outside in the hotel garden, Madame Poisson was

standing with Toto on the end of a lead. She looked pale and agitated.

'Madame!' cried Violet. 'Is something wrong?'

The little governess shook her head, although Violet could see she was near to tears. And from past experience Violet knew that the only person who could upset Madame Poisson like that was her mother.

'Has Lady Eleanor spoken to you this morning?'

'Indeed, yes, Violette,' replied the governess. 'Your poor mother was most out of sorts. She was obliged to wait for Madame Duchamps, only to discover that the lady and her husband have left Monte Carlo for Paris on urgent business.'

Violet understood immediately that her mother had taken out her irritation on her poor governess. 'So she was angry with you?'

'Not *angry*, my dear.' Madam Poisson fiddled miserably with her faded pink cloche hat. 'She merely suggested that I visit the milliner's without delay.'

'So you won't be coming with me to visit Lady Caroline,' said Violet gently.

Madame Poisson shook her head. 'However, your mother is quite right,' she said with a rueful smile. 'This is the hat of a scarecrow. But it is not only for that reason that I cannot accompany you. It is because of Her Ladyship's bloodhounds.'

'I beg your pardon?'

'I have received a strange note, warning me about these dogs,' explained the little governess, her eyes wide and bulging. 'Apparently they are very big and very fierce and they never leave Lady Caroline's side!'

Violet knew her dear codfish was terrified of large dogs. 'But they're bloodhounds, Madame,' she said. 'Bloodhounds aren't fierce.'

The governess's eyes went round and popped out more than ever. 'But they slobber, Violette. I know they do.' She stared anxiously into Violet's face. 'You do not mind going to visit Her Ladyship on your own, do you?'

'Of course not,' said Violet quickly. 'One of the boys from the hotel will come with me.'

Violet had never seen her governess in such a state. She guessed it must also be because of her worry about the family farm. Her codfish had become more and more preoccupied since they had arrived in France. Once again she was tempted to offer to speak to her father – anything to reassure her dear codfish –

but she remembered the conversation with Garth on the train. Both her father and her governess would be cross with her for interfering. It was best to let things take their course.

'Don't you worry about me, Madame,' said Violet. 'But if you could look after Toto, I would be very grateful.' She kissed her governess on the cheek. 'I'm sure he hates big dogs as much as you do.'

Violet had a plan of her own. If Madame Poisson wasn't with her she could cut her visit to Lady Caroline short without anyone suggesting she was being rude. Then she could be back at the hotel when Garth returned from his pigeon-shooting to tell him what she had overheard the Countess saying to the hotel manager.

They would unravel the mystery yet!

Lady Caroline Egmont lived in a villa called Le Soleil, that looked like a gigantic wedding cake set in the middle of terraced olive trees in the hills behind Monte Carlo. The pony trotted through the gates and stopped outside the front door. Violet stepped down from the trap onto the white, dusty forecourt. She had prepared herself for a tedious conversation over a cup of tea, followed by an elaborate tour of the garden.

To her surprise, a young girl in a maid's uniform appeared at the door and ran towards her. She curtsied and introduced herself as Eloise, Lady Caroline's maid, and told Violet that her mistress was shooting pigeons in the hills behind the house and had asked that Violet join her immediately.

'What?' gasped Violet. She was so taken aback that for a moment all she could do was stare at the maid's tanned, serious face.

'Come,' said Eloise urgently, taking the basket of fish from her, 'Lady Caroline does not like to be kept waiting.'

The next minute Violet was walking up a stony track behind the stables at the back of the villa. They turned a corner and she saw a short, stocky woman standing in the middle of a terrace. She guessed it must be Lady Caroline because there were two enormous bloodhounds standing by her, and she had a shotgun in her hand.

Violet wiped a sheen of perspiration from her face with a cotton handkerchief. Even though it was a warm morning, Lady Caroline was dressed in thick tweeds. Violet heard the sound of men shouting in the bushes. Then three pigeons fluttered into the sky. Lady Caroline turned, aimed and fired. Three loud bangs ricocheted around the hills.

A keeper waved them forward and Violet crossed over and introduced herself.

'Delighted. Welcome to Le Soleil.' Lady Caroline had the look of a terrier and spoke in short bursts. 'You shoot, of course?'

'Only once,' replied Violet hesitantly. 'My father taught me.'

Lady Caroline chortled. '*I* taught *him*.' She peered at Violet and seemed to approve of what she saw. Percy had been wise when he wrote to arrange the visit. Violet took after him, not his wife, and he knew perfectly well that Her Ladyship didn't hold with beauties. They were like racehorses – unpredictable and highly strung.

She nodded to a keeper, who handed Violet a beautifully worked double-barrelled shotgun. 'Try this. It's light and well balanced. Practically fires itself.'

Violet held the gun in her hands and felt her heart banging in her chest. Now she was terrified she was going to make a fool of herself.

'Don't you worry,' said Lady Caroline, guessing her

thoughts. 'It's the last beat of the morning.' She smiled at Violet's anxious face. 'Bet you were cross when you were left at the hotel this morning while the men went out shooting without you.'

Now Violet was flabbergasted. 'How did you know?'

'Your father told me when he wrote,' replied Lady Caroline. 'He said you'd been doing the rounds of dull society daughters, so we concocted a scheme. Only I didn't want that pop-eyed governess of yours, too.'

'*You* told Madame Poisson about the bloodhounds?' asked Violet.

'Wrote the note myself.' Lady Caroline allowed herself a moment of triumph. 'Of course, they're not fierce at all, but I wanted to meet Percy's gel on my own.'

Lady Caroline held up her hand. Half a dozen beaters began to shout and hit the bushes with sticks again. The next moment, several pigeons flew into the air.

'Yours!' cried Lady Caroline.

Violet fired and, to her utter amazement, two birds fluttered to the ground.

'Fine shot!' cried Lady Caroline.

For one dreadful moment, Violet thought Lady Caroline was going to kiss her. But she was wrong. The next moment, Her Ladyship brought down two birds herself.

An hour later, Violet was sitting in a large dining room with a bloodhound called Thunder resting his head on her feet.

'Ever eaten an ostrich-egg soufflé?' asked Lady Caroline. 'I keep a flock up the back. Reminds me. Must send you back with some feathers for your mother.' She smiled at Violet. 'Thank you for the fish, by the way. Nothing like a finnan haddie.'

At that moment, a maid set down a golden soufflé on the table and spooned it onto Violet's plate. When they had both been served, Violet swallowed a forkful. It was delicious.

She looked across to where Lady Caroline was surreptitiously holding out a piece of bread for her other bloodhound, Lightning. Violet had never felt so completely at ease so quickly with anyone before. Lady Caroline could almost have been her grandmother.

'I've had a glorious morning,' said Violet. 'Thank you.'

'You're good company, my dear,' replied Lady Caroline. 'Like your father was at your age.' She paused and looked at Violet with her raisin-brown eyes. 'Ever seen an ostrich face to face?'

'Only through bars at the zoo.'

'Stupid birds, of course. Brain the size of a bantam.' Lady Caroline dabbed at her mouth with her napkin. 'You ride, of course?'

Violet laughed with pure pleasure. 'I *love* riding.'

'Then we'll try you on Tempest. He's a stallion but I'd say you can handle him.'

Violet rested her hands on Tempest's saddle and let the warm breeze dry the sweat in her hair. The stallion lowered his powerful neck and nibbled at the rough grass at his feet. Beside her, Lady Caroline sat back in her stirrups. Neither of them was riding side-saddle, which would have shocked her mother and Madame Poisson. In fact, just about everything Violet had done that day would have shocked her mother and her governess.

It was too wonderful for words!

Violet looked down over the terraces of twisted olive trees to where the land dropped into the sparkling sea. The sound of the bloodhounds baying drifted up from the dense undergrowth of thorny-leaved bushes.

'After a rabbit,' said Lady Caroline. 'Thunder picks up the trail and Lightning stays with it.'

'Why did you give them those names?'

'Always call my animals after extreme weather,' replied Lady Caroline, smiling. She turned her horse round and they headed slowly back down the hill. 'Now, tell me, what do you think of Monte Carlo?'

Rather than answering Lady Caroline's question, Violet found herself thinking of what she had overheard that morning in the hotel's front hall. Why had the Countess claimed a friendship with her parents that didn't exist? It occurred to Violet that her hostess might know of the Drakensburgs, and, indeed, the Duchamps. She seemed to know all the regular visitors.

Lady Caroline gave Violet a quizzical look. 'Is something worrying you, my dear?'

'Just something odd, that's all,' replied Violet, and she told Lady Caroline about the thefts at the Ritz, the Duchamps, the Countess's strange behaviour at dinner the night before they left and the conversation about paste diamonds with Marie. Finally she mentioned what she had heard the Countess say that morning.

'I've never heard of a Monsieur and Madame Duchamps or, indeed, a Count and Countess Drakensburg in Monte Carlo,' said Lady Caroline as they stopped in front of the stables. 'Not that that means anything, of course. The town is full of charlatans, and Russian aristocrats pop up overnight like mushrooms.' She paused and looked at Violet with thoughtful eyes. 'But I should have a word with your mother and father about Lady Eleanor's diamonds. It's no shame to wear paste. Only common sense, in fact.'

A groom rushed forward to hold their horses and Violet slid down and stamped her boots on the dusty ground. She tried to imagine her mother using ordinary common sense. It was easier to imagine snow in the desert.

SEVEN

'An ostrich-egg *soufflé*?' cried Garth incredulously, as Violet described her day with Lady Caroline Egmont. 'What did it taste like?'

'Delicious,' replied Violet. 'And then we went riding on stallions.' She paused and tried not to sound smug. 'What was *your* day like?'

Garth pulled a face. 'Full of boring old men. Except for Frank Winalot, of course. Henri Duchamps wasn't there – he had to leave Monte Carlo for urgent business in Paris, apparently. That Count Drakensburg arrived and took his place. Your father didn't seem too pleased to see him, though.'

Violet shrugged. 'Maybe he was annoyed because

the Duchamps disappeared without any notice. Mother was very cross and took it out on the poor codfish.'

At that moment, Lady Eleanor swept into the drawing room where they were sitting. 'Violet, my dear,' she cried, smiling. 'I've just received the sweetest note from Caroline Egmont. She said you were absolutely charming.' Lady Eleanor bent down and kissed Violet on the cheek. 'So kind of you, darling. I know it was a tedious errand to visit her today.'

'Not at all, Mother,' replied Violet. 'Lady Caroline is—'

'So, as a thank-you present,' interrupted Lady Eleanor, 'your father and I thought we would take you and Garth to the casino tonight!' Lady Eleanor beamed. 'We are to be the guests of Ivan and Juliet Drakensburg. Juliet mentioned she saw you this morning. I told her you were on your way to visit Caroline Egmont, which is doubtless why you didn't introduce yourself.' Lady Eleanor sighed happily. 'Dear Juliet! She is such a kind, sweet creature. And so concerned for Mrs Stuyvesant Fish.'

Violet's heart was thumping as her mother went on talking. So the Countess *had* seen her after all. She must have eyes in the back of her head. And it must have been perfectly clear that Violet had been avoiding her.

'And Violet, darling –' Lady Eleanor stood up from where she had perched on the edge of the sofa – '*do* try and look your best tonight. *Everyone* will be there.'

As Violet watched her mother leave the room, she suddenly remembered Lady Caroline's advice about not wearing real diamonds. She turned to Garth. 'Where's my father?'

'He went to the Café de Paris with Frank,' said Garth. 'What's wrong?'

Violet slumped back on the sofa and told Garth what she had overheard the Countess say to the hotel manager that morning and what Lady Caroline had said about not wearing real diamonds.

'There's no point in *me* saying anything to Mother,' said Violet. 'She'd never listen, and we still don't know if they're up to anything yet.'

'No,' agreed Garth. 'And she'd probably tell the Countess.'

Violet stared at him. 'There *is* something peculiar about that woman, isn't there? I mean, first she pretends to know Mrs Stuyvesant Fish really well and now she's doing the same thing with my mother.'

'I wonder if they ever met the Duchamps,' said Garth thoughtfully.

'What do you mean?'

'I don't know. I'm just trying to think it through. Everywhere they've turned up, someone's jewellery has been stolen.' Garth paused. 'I don't like to admit it, but what Marie said about bad guys looking like good guys might actually be right.'

'So you think the robberies at the Ritz were an inside job?'

'How do I know?' replied Garth. 'All I'm saying is that it's an odd coincidence that the same people have turned up here.' He looked into Violet's serious eyes. 'I think you should tell your father what Lady Caroline said.'

'Are you suggesting my mother could be next on the list?'

Garth shrugged. 'Who knows? But at least we can keep our eyes peeled now that we have our suspicions.'

'Lady Caroline did say that Monte Carlo was full of charlatans. So did Marie, for that matter.' Violet heaved herself up from the deep feather cushions of the sofa and stared ahead gloomily as a procession of women left the room to dress for the evening. 'I hate dressing up.'

'Chin up, old girl,' Garth said in his worst English accent. 'It'll be fun to see the casino and it's all in the line of duty.' He raised an eyebrow. 'Besides, I bet I win more than you tonight!'

'Garth!' cried Violet, pretending to be shocked. 'You know perfectly well I don't gamble!'

'Huh,' said Garth as Violet turned away, 'we'll see about that!'

To Violet, the casino looked like a fairy-tale palace, perched over the sea, set in its own gardens of palm trees and spiky-leaved bushes sprouting bright red flowers.

Their cab wound up the raked gravel drive and stopped outside the main entrance. A footman dressed in a black and yellow uniform opened the door. Lord Percy leaned forward with his top hat in his hand and stepped down from the dark velvet interior of the cab. Garth followed quickly after him. Then another footman helped down Lady Eleanor and Violet.

For a moment, they stood together among the marble pillars of the brightly lit portico. Lady Eleanor was brilliant under the electric lamps. Her dress was grey silk shot through with silver thread, its low bodice masked with silver lace. But the *real* brilliance was her jewellery. A vast square diamond pendant fixed in an intricate platinum setting hung around her neck, while long diamond earrings sparkled at her ears.

There were other ladies all around them, each one just as beautifully dressed and glittering with jewels. Marie was right. Without a magnifying glass, you could not tell which jewels were real and which were fake. And even then you would have to know what you were looking for.

'How exciting!' cried Lady Eleanor. She patted her sequined purse and walked quickly through the double doors into the front hall on Lord Percy's arm.

The first thing that struck Violet as she followed her parents into the huge hall was the atmosphere in the crowd. It was unbelievably tense and brittle, as if everyone was caught up in a frenzy of anticipation. Even her own parents seemed affected by it. Violet watched as they made their way through the crowd like clockwork dolls. They were stiff and edgy, stopping and talking in short bursts of animated conversation with smiles that seemed too wide and hand gestures that looked almost jerky.

'Wow!' whispered Garth in her ear. 'No wonder people go crazy here. It's like the starting gate at a horse race.'

As they stood to one side, the crowd moved across the huge hall towards the gaming room. It was as if they were being drawn by some invisible magnet.

Garth and Violet found themselves being swept along too, and a moment later they were in a vast room with fat pillars and a high, gilded ceiling.

'This must be the main gambling saloon,' said Garth.

Violet nodded. Her parents had vanished into the crowd.

Now Violet had time to look around, she couldn't believe her eyes. It was like standing in the drawing room of a huge country house where a ball was taking place. The walls were painted the palest turquoise and covered with paintings of Greek gods and goddesses. Gold cherubs sprang from elaborate plasterwork and gilt mirrors made the room look even bigger than it was. Two great chandeliers hung from the high ceilings. But there the similarity with a country house ended.

Underneath the chandeliers, lit by their hard, bright light were three enormous tables, each with its own roulette wheel set in a brass mount in the middle. Hundreds of richly dressed men and women clustered around the tables like bees around pools of honey. Over the noise of voices, Violet could clearly hear the rattle of the spinning balls and the *clack* of counters being stacked and raked in.

At each table, four croupiers stood still as statues, their voices intoning the same instructions over and over again. *Mesdames et Messieurs, faîtes vos jeux. Les jeux sont faits, rien ne va plus.* But even though their bodies hardly ever moved, their eyes never stayed still.

Violet and Garth watched as the croupier at the table in front of them leaned over and spun the wheel. Each time he did this the crowd held its breath as the ball jumped from red to black and number to number, then, slowly, slowly, the wheel finally stopped spinning and the ball settled.

'This is giving me the creeps,' said Garth as some people gasped in horror and hid their faces, while others squealed with triumph.

At that moment, there was a great roar from the next-door room.

'They're playing *trente et quarante*,' explained Violet. 'My father told me it's the rich man's card game.' She jerked her head towards the roulette wheel. 'This is "Snap" by comparison.'

Out of the corner of her eye, Violet saw her mother. She was laughing, her face lit up with a sort of wild glee. It was an expression Violet had never seen before and she began to feel more and more uncomfortable.

Another roar came from the next-door room.

'Come on,' said Garth. 'Let's find out what's going on. I bet the room's full of diamond thieves.'

'Have you seen what my mother's wearing?'

'I'd be blind not to.'

Violet and Garth walked into the next-door room just in time to see Ivan Drakensburg stand up from a green-baize table marked out on the edges with a red and black diamond.

As he stood up, the Countess joined him. She was

wearing a scarlet evening dress and her dark red hair was pinned up with jewelled black ostrich feathers. She made Violet think of the queen of spades.

The Count kissed his wife's hand and stepped back from the table. There was an enormous pile of red chips in front of him. He must have made a fortune! Then, to Violet's horror, she saw her mother hurry across the parquet floor and kiss him. Suddenly a crowd began to form around them.

Violet looked away. 'How much did he win?'

'One million francs,' said Garth, who had been listening to the excited chatter around the table. 'All red cards, apparently.' As he spoke, he saw the Count being escorted through a side door as hundreds of people followed him, all trying to shake his hand or touch his evening jacket.

'What's going on?' asked Violet.

'Gamblers think that luck's catching,' replied Garth. 'Everyone wants it.'

Violet felt a great surge of disgust and turned furiously away.

'Get a grip, Vi, for heaven's sake,' said Garth, putting his hand on her shoulder. 'Your mother and the Countess are heading straight for us.'

Violet took one look at her mother's face and ran from the room.

Outside on the balcony, she stood and stared over the sparkling silver sea. The breeze made her feel better. It was her mother's face that had upset her so much. It was almost *glistening* with something that looked very much like greed. And where was her father? Perhaps he was gambling in another room.

Violet took a deep breath to steady her nerves. She knew she had to go back into the casino and find Garth. It was crazy not to. Now that all the talk was of the Count winning such a fortune, this was their chance to find out what they could about the Drakensburgs.

At that moment, Violet looked down and her heart banged in her chest. If it hadn't been a full moon, she would never have seen him. Yet there was Henri Duchamps, supposedly in Paris on urgent business, walking through the gardens below her.

Violet watched as he circled a large spiky bush and, with a quick look over his shoulder, ran down the steps to the promenade below and set off into the night.

'Feeling better?' Garth asked, appearing at her side.

'I told your mother the heat was making you feel faint.'

'Thanks.' Violet paused. 'I've just seen Henri Duchamps.'

'That's impossible! They're in Paris.'

Violet pointed down to the garden. 'He just went down the steps onto the promenade.'

Suddenly Violet decided she couldn't face the casino again. 'I'm going back to the hotel. I'll take Toto for a walk.'

'But it's almost ten o'clock!'

'So what?' Violet looked over her shoulder. 'I'd say my parents are there for the evening and I could do with some air.'

'The point is, Vi,' said Garth as they walked through the hotel gardens with Toto dancing along on his lead, 'all gamblers are secretive. They have to be. And they're always sniffing about for information. I guess that's what Henri Duchamps was up to.'

'I think there's more to it,' said Violet. 'I mean, why would the Duchamps – and the Drakensburgs, for that matter – be so keen to pretend they're friends with people they don't even know?'

Garth shrugged. 'Search me. Maybe they're both crooks who want to steal from the aristocrats.' He shook his head. 'But the Count has just won a fortune. Why would he want more?'

'I'm sure some people *like* stealing,' replied Violet. 'Like some people can't stop gambling.'

'What on earth are you two doing out at this time of night?' It was a loud male voice, with an American accent.

Frank and Lily Winalot were standing in front of them on the promenade. Garth and Violet had been so busy talking they had almost bumped into them.

'Violet and Garth are taking the air, Frank, like us,' said Lily. 'Honestly, you do sound like an old fuddy-duddy. This *is* Monte Carlo. Some people stay up all night.'

'Not me,' said Frank. 'Call me old-fashioned, but *I* say it's time for a hot chocolate.' He turned to Violet and Garth. 'Would you two care to join us?'

'We'd love to,' said Violet, with a sudden rush of relief.

'We saw Garth earlier at the casino,' said Lily, hearing the emotion in Violet's voice. She reached out and

105

touched her hand. 'He said you didn't like it much.'

'Worse than a bear pit,' muttered Frank.

Violet pulled a face. 'Give me a bear pit any day.'

Frank put his arm through Violet's. 'Spoken like a true American,' he said, laughing.

And for the first time that evening, Violet laughed too.

EIGHT

The next morning, at breakfast, Garth and Violet were reading the *Monte Carlo Gazette* and poking fun at a visitor called Lady Celia Dawson, who had insisted on dressing up as Joan of Arc on her social calls, when Lord Percy walked into the dining room.

Violet took one look at his face and her stomach turned over.

'Father—'

But Lord Percy held up his hand for silence. 'There's been a robbery,' he said. 'Your mother's diamond necklace and her engagement ring have been stolen.'

'Oh no!' cried Violet. 'When?'

'It must have happened during the night.' Lord Percy looked around the room at the other guests, who were talking and drinking their morning coffee. 'But it is essential we are discreet. The thieves could be anywhere.'

'Surely whoever stole Her Ladyship's jewels will already have left Monte Carlo,' said Garth.

'Not necessarily,' replied Lord Percy. 'The *gendarmes* believe it could be an inside job.'

'You mean dishonest staff?' asked Violet.

'I mean dishonest *people*,' replied her father. 'Staff or guests. No one knows, which is why you mustn't say anything to anybody. The *gendarmes* expect another robbery.'

Violet could hardly imagine how her mother must be feeling. Her engagement ring was her most precious jewel – almost a part of her. She was always twisting it around her finger. 'How is Mother?' asked Violet anxiously.

'Distraught,' said Lord Percy. 'You know how attached she is to her ring.' He rested his hand on Violet's shoulder. 'She's been given a sedative for her nerves. As soon as she is in better spirits, I'll tell you.'

Violet slumped in her chair.

'Lady Caroline asked me to warn Mother about jewel thieves,' she whispered to her father. 'But by the time I remembered . . .'

Lord Percy looked into his daughter's unhappy face. 'Do you think I didn't warn her myself?' He paused. 'She feels absolutely dreadful now.'

'Is there anything we can do to help?' asked Garth.

'Indeed there is, Garth,' replied Lord Percy. 'I almost forgot.' He felt in his pocket and took out a letter. 'Would you see this reaches Countess Drakensburg? Lady Eleanor has had to cancel their visit to Grasse.'

Garth took the letter. 'Does the Countess know about the theft?'

Lord Percy was looking out of the window and didn't seem to be listening.

Garth repeated his question.

'*Nobody* knows,' said Lord Percy. 'And, as I said, it must stay that way.' He turned abruptly. 'I'll see you both at tea.'

Violet was so startled by her father's sudden disappearance that she found herself staring at her mother's copperplate handwriting on the thick vellum envelope. 'He's not telling us something,' she said, half to herself. 'He knows more than he's saying.'

But Garth wasn't listening. 'Don't turn round,' he said in a low voice. 'The Duchamps have just walked in and they're heading straight for us.'

As Violet looked up, a strange thought occurred to her. Had her father seen the Duchamps through the hotel window? Were *they* the reason he had left so quickly?

'Violet! Garth!' Florence Duchamps took their hands in her cold, slimy grasp. 'I'm so glad we've found you both. Your dear parents must have thought we had quite disappeared, Violet!'

'We understood you were in Paris,' said Violet, in a puzzled voice.

Florence Duchamps turned to her husband with a look of astonishment. 'Really, Henri! Did you ever hear such fairy stories?'

Henri Duchamps shook his head. 'Another silly rumour, my dear. Monte Carlo is thick with them.' He turned to Violet. 'How is your dear mother? We've heard of her dreadful loss, of course.'

Violet coughed to hide her surprise. How on earth

had the Duchamps found out about the theft when so far no one but her own family knew?

'We may be able to help,' continued Florence Duchamps in a pressing voice.

'Have they arrested the thieves in Paris?' asked Garth, to cover Violet's surprise, even though he was just as taken aback.

'Not yet,' replied Henri. 'But they have pretty firm suspicions.'

'Henri and I would very much like to offer any comfort we can to your dear mother,' said Florence in the same quiet, insistent voice.

'I'm afraid she cannot be disturbed,' said Violet.

Florence Duchamps nodded. 'Poor dear Eleanor. Please pass on our concerns.'

'Thank you,' said Violet. She looked innocently at Florence Duchamps's face with its slash of red lipstick. 'But may I ask how you know of my mother's loss?'

A flicker of surprise passed over Florence's face. Then Henri Duchamps said smoothly, 'Why, your father wrote to us this morning.'

'Surely he mentioned it to you?' said Florence, looking at Violet with a steady gaze.

It was all getting rather uncomfortable as far as

Garth was concerned. 'Lord Percy was in quite a state when we spoke this morning,' he said.

'Of course.' Florence stood up and took her husband's arm. 'Well, goodbye, my dears.' And with that, they walked out of the room.

Both Garth and Violet got up and walked over to the window to see if the Duchamps would leave the hotel, but after waiting for five minutes there was still no sign of them walking down the wide entrance steps.

'Perhaps they went through the back garden,' said Violet, reading Garth's mind. 'There's another entrance, you know.'

'Of course I know,' said Garth sharply. 'Oh, sorry, Vi. I didn't mean—'

'Don't worry,' interrupted Violet. 'They're lying. My father's lying, too. Let's go back to the casino. It would be useful to know if Henri Duchamps went inside last night. His name will be in the visitor's book.'

'What about your fish-head governess?' said Garth. 'You'll have to tell her something.'

'I'm just about to,' replied Violet. 'It goes like this: Toto needs a walk.' She stopped and looked at Garth.

'It's strange, every time I go to her room, she's playing some sort of game with a pack of cards and a note-book.'

Garth shrugged. 'Maybe she thinks she's got a win-ning system. Everyone else does in this town.'

'The codfish would never gamble.'

'You said that about your parents,' replied Garth. 'Crazy things happen in crazy places. Anyway, I'll give the Countess her letter and meet you in the hall.'

Five minutes later Violet walked into the hall with Toto in her arms and saw Garth standing white-faced by the front door. 'The Count and Countess have left the hotel,' he said, shaking his head. 'They took the train to Vienna early this morning.'

'*What?*' cried Violet, astonished. She clipped on Toto's lead and walked down the front steps to the promenade. 'But the Countess had arranged a visit to look at some perfume factories this afternoon with my mother. It was the appointment she was cancelling in her letter.' She paused. 'Did they leave a note?'

'Nothing.'

'Then my father doesn't know either.'

'I'm sure he would have said.'

Violet frowned. 'There's something strange going on. I don't believe for one moment that my father wrote to the Duchamps.'

'In which case it was a pretty stupid lie, because all we have to do is ask him,' said Garth.

'Maybe I should do that now,' said Violet.

Garth shook his head. 'I'd leave him alone for the moment. He has a lot on his mind and I got the strong impression that the reason he left us so quickly was because he saw the Duchamps through the window.'

'I thought so too,' said Violet.

'Why so glum, my treasured companions?' Marie Cherkassky appeared from behind a potted palm tree, her black eyes gleaming in her pudgy face. 'Tell your friend Marie your troubles.' She thumped her chest with her hand. 'She will solve them for you! Every one!'

Marie stared at Garth's and Violet's startled faces. 'What, no reply? I am an ogre, yes?'

Violet took one look at Garth's furious face and spoke before he had a chance to agree wholeheartedly. 'How lovely to see you, Marie,' she gabbled as she kissed the young Russian's cheek. 'But what have you done with your poor governess?'

'I gave her the, uh, yes, *slip* at the train station,' cried Marie proudly. She stopped at the look on their faces. 'Or do I mean *petticoat*?'

'When you were at the station?' asked Violet and Garth at the same time.

'Early this morning, of course,' replied Marie, looking puzzled. 'My mother and sister go to Vienna to see the banker, Omotov.' She shrugged. 'Since my father cannot find his pen to write cheque, we have no money.'

'Did you see Count and Countess Drakensburg?' asked Violet quickly. 'She's tall with dark red hair and—'

'They were on the same train,' interrupted Garth.

'I know them but I don't see them.' Marie's eyes glittered angrily. 'My mother visits them. Always we Russians help each other.' Suddenly she stamped her foot. 'And you guess what?'

'What?' cried Violet.

Marie stamped her foot again, as if she was too angry to speak.

'Tell us, Marie,' said Garth impatiently.

'They are not *Russians*,' said Marie, almost spitting out her words.

'How do you know?' asked Garth.

'They do not help pay for my piano! And I a prodigy!' Marie began to pace back and forth, waving her arms in the air. 'I told you, always Russians help each other!'

'So now my dear mother goes to Vienna to beg from Banker Omotov. So I make telephone call to my friend in Paris who knows all Russians.' Marie took a deep breath. 'He says, "What is this name Drakensburg? Not Russian name. Never heard of them. It is to fool silly people, Marie."

'So!' Marie stood in front of them and folded her arms. 'They are like the paste I tell you about. They are fakes.'

Before Violet could even begin to take in what Marie had just said, a clock rang out eleven times. 'Oh, no!' she cried. 'I completely forgot. I have to meet Lily Winalot in ten minutes!'

Suddenly a brilliant idea occurred to her. 'Can you ride, Marie?'

'Naturally,' replied Marie. 'I ride the horse like a genius.'

'Excellent,' said Violet to Marie. 'Let's get you back to our hotel before Madame Tanenko tracks you down.'

Marie whooped with delight and clapped her hands. 'An adventure!' she cried. 'How tremendously jolly exciting!'

'What about me?' demanded Garth, trying to not feel left out. 'I'm coming too!'

Violet burst out laughing. 'Garth, you goof! You don't know how to ride!'

'So what?' asked Garth, grinning. 'There's a first time for everyone!'

Two hours later, Garth was beginning to wish he had never set eyes on a horse, let alone climbed on top of one. Of course, Violet and Lily had cantered on ahead almost immediately and now every muscle in his body ached. Worse, whenever the horse broke into a trot or, for one truly terrifying moment, a canter, he was sure he would fall off and break his neck. It was only by leaning forward and clutching onto the horse's mane that he stopped himself from tumbling to the ground.

The only *good* thing about the whole experience

was that it was perfectly clear that Marie was no better than he was. Far from being a genius on a horse, she barely knew one end from the other. 'I can only ride white horses,' complained Marie in a bad-tempered voice after they had agreed to stick to a slow walk. 'This black beast is all wrong. He swing about like fairground chair.'

Garth resisted the temptation to tease her and instead decided to tell her about the Drakensburgs' mysterious disappearance from the hotel that morning. She was such a strange girl, she might just have a good idea about tracking them down. 'Since you didn't see them at the station, we don't know whether they've *really* gone to Vienna or not,' he added.

'Why you not bribe the hotel porter,' replied Marie. 'Maybe he see something that tell you more. They must leave from front door? Yes? So he see them.' She shifted uncomfortably on the back of her horse. 'People see all kinds of things when the money has cleaned their eyes, you know.' She grinned at him. 'Why, I have idea to bribe *you* right now!'

'What about?'

'About this torture, of course,' said Marie, waving her gloved hand at the horse's head. 'Why not we turn back? I for my piano lesson and you to bribe porter.'

'But what about Violet and Lily?' asked Garth. 'Won't they worry?'

Marie snorted. 'They don't worry leaving us behind hours ago. Why they worry if we go home?'

Garth grinned. He had to admit he was growing rather fond of this crazy Russian girl. And maybe she wasn't so daft after all. 'Best news I've heard all day,' he said. And, without thinking, he dug his heels into the side of his horse and it took off at a fast trot.

The last thing Garth remembered hearing before he slid ignominiously off the saddle and into the bushes was the sound of Marie's hysterical laughter.

Later that afternoon, as Garth described his first and last attempt at riding a horse, Violet poured out a cup of the Earl Grey tea that Lady Eleanor had brought especially from London. 'So, did the porter see anything?'

'He said the Countess was picked up by a chauffeured car at six o'clock this morning.' Garth paused. 'Apparently her chauffeur was reading an *English* newspaper.'

'What's so important about that?' asked Violet, puzzled.

Garth reached across the table and put an almond biscuit in his mouth. 'The chauffeurs around here are all French, and peasant French, too, so that's why the porter noticed. I mean, how many bilingual chauffeurs do you hear of?' He gulped his tea. 'The porter also noticed that this chauffeur looked impatient and annoyed, because he was drumming his fingers on his lapels, which isn't exactly the behaviour of your normal chauffeur, either. Chauffeurs aren't paid to get impatient.'

Garth swallowed another biscuit. 'I mean, why should it matter to him whether his mistress misses her train or not? He's there to wait.'

'Did the porter actually see the Countess get into the car?'

'No. He had to do something in the hotel. By the time he was back at his post, the car had gone.'

Violet swallowed her tea and poured out another cup for both of them. Then she said thoughtfully, 'Let's pretend for the moment that your hunch is right and the Count and Countess *are* somehow involved with the robberies. Maybe this unlikely chauffeur is their accomplice. Maybe he is the professional safe-cracker with friends in all the fancy hotels. Everyone seems to think it's an inside job, and certainly that would explain why the Countess was so put out at dinner when Mrs Stuyvesant Fish said she had changed her plans.'

'I'm not following you,' said Garth, whose legs were aching so much he could hardly think straight.

'Look at it this way,' said Violet. 'Imagine the Count and Countess had already robbed the Duchamps and targeted Mrs Stuyvesant Fish. They wouldn't want to strike again so quickly, so they went about trying to ask her to the opera and set up a friendship so that no one could suspect them. Then everything went wrong. The moment they knew Mrs Stuyvesant Fish was leaving the next day, they had to change their plans. And guess what, the jewellery disappeared that night.'

Violet rubbed her hands over her face and tried to keep her train of thought going. 'Then suddenly they appear in Monte Carlo. Remember they have seen my mother's diamonds at the Ritz. Within forty-eight hours, she is robbed and the Drakensburgs disappear, along with this chauffeur who reads English newspapers.'

121

'I don't know,' said Garth slowly. 'It all sounds a bit far-fetched to me. Maybe I'm wrong but I think they'll be back at the end of the week. Perhaps Marie is just spreading rumours about them because they wouldn't give her mother any money to help her pay for the piano.' He chewed on another biscuit. 'Did you find out anything from Lily?'

'Yes,' said Violet. 'And it makes it even more difficult to work out if either of them is the thief.'

'Try me.'

'According to Frank Winalot, Henri Duchamps cheats at cards.'

'Not exactly gentlemanly behaviour.'

'Quite. So I asked Lily if Frank had mentioned this to anyone else, like my father for instance, and Lily said she thought it unlikely, since Frank doesn't know him that well. And as it stands, Frank has no proof, only suspicions.'

'Sounds familiar,' said Garth.

'Well, it's too late now.' Violet spread out her hands. 'While you were sitting in your bath, my father told me that he's taking my mother to Italy for a few days. They left half an hour ago.'

'Seems like a good idea to me,' said Garth.

'So far,' said Violet drily.

Garth looked up. 'So, what comes next?'

'You won't like this and nor do I. Florence Duchamps managed to get in to see my mother. The Italian trip was her suggestion.' Violet stared at her hands. 'The upshot of it is that they offered to act as our guardians while Mother and Father are away – and their offer was accepted.'

Garth flushed with anger. 'The *Duchamps!*' He practically spat out the name. 'I'll have nothing to do with them!'

'For heaven's sake, calm down,' said Violet. 'We'll use the time to spy on them.'

'What's wrong with old fish-face?' demanded Garth. 'It's always been her job before.'

Violet picked up her cup. Suddenly her hand shook so much the tea slopped into the saucer.

'Vi!' cried Garth. 'What is it?'

A shudder went through Violet's body. 'That awful Duchamps woman told my mother she had seen Madame at the casino!'

Garth frowned. 'But surely Madame Poisson can do what she likes in her spare time.'

'Apparently not,' replied Violet. 'My mother

123

wanted to sack her immediately but my father refused.'

'That's a bit rich coming from your mother after the other night at the casino.'

'Quite,' said Violet. 'But the thing is, I suddenly remembered all the times I'd found Madame with a pack of cards and a list of numbers in a notebook.' She stared into Garth's face. 'Maybe she really *is* taking this gambling thing seriously, in which case she could lose all of her savings. Anything could happen! She's so worried about her family, she's not thinking straight.' Violet shook her head. 'I don't understand why my father hasn't spoken to her yet about Les Pradelles.'

'Nor do I. I did mention it the other day and all he said was that it was in hand.' Garth looked up. 'And it was pretty clear he didn't appreciate my concern. So, what's going to happen to the codfish?'

'They agreed on a compromise. Madame has been sent back to Paris for a week. Hence the Duchamps taking her place.'

Violet turned away so that Garth wouldn't see the tears in her eyes.

For a moment, neither spoke.

'OK, partner,' said Garth at last. He reached out and touched Violet's arm. 'This is the plan. We give the Duchamps the petticoat, as your friend Marie says, and we find out who's behind these thefts. You get your mother's engagement ring back and *kapow!* she owes you one and leaves the codfish alone for ever!' He threw up his arms and grinned. *'Whaddyathink?'*

'We'll do it,' said Violet. Suddenly she grinned, too. 'We've done it before and we'll do it again. We darned well will!'

NINE

Lady Caroline Egmont didn't often go into Monte Carlo. She preferred the company of her books and her dogs to that of the people who packed out the cafés and talked endlessly of foolproof systems to win at cards or predict the spin of the roulette wheel.

As far as she was concerned, gambling was a fool's game. The only certainty was that the casino would get their money back sooner or later. But she was fond of Lord Percy and had taken a great liking to Violet since the afternoon they had spent together. Of course, she'd never had much time for Lady Eleanor, but still, she had been kind enough to remember her basket of smoked haddock and the least Lady Caroline could do was thank her.

Now, as the cab moved briskly down the promenade, Lady Caroline was out of sorts and troubled. She had called at the Hermitage only to discover that the Winters were in Italy, and that Violet and their American ward, Garth Hudson, were in the charge of Madame and Monsieur Duchamps.

Lady Caroline gazed out of the cab window. She prided herself on her memory and she recalled quite clearly her conversation with Violet when the name of this rather dubious-sounding couple had been mentioned, along with an equally dubious Count and Countess Drakensburg. The old lady frowned. What on earth had persuaded Percy Winters to leave his daughter and his ward in such unsuitable hands?

At that moment, she saw Violet and a tall young man walking down the promenade beside an older man and woman. She was sure from Violet's description that they must be the Duchamps and she took an instant dislike to them.

The woman had a figure like a boy's, blonde, bobbed hair and a vulgar outfit in the new tailored fashion. The man's check suit was altogether too loud and his homburg hat was totally unsuitable. As if that wasn't bad enough, the furious expression on Violet's face confirmed Lady Caroline's suspicions.

The four of them crossed the street and walked over to the forecourt of the Café de Paris and through the double doors.

Lady Caroline didn't normally approve of snap decisions, but she made one now. She lifted her stick and tapped sharply on the roof of her cab.

The cab stopped and the driver jumped down and opened the door.

'Wait for me here, Marcel,' said Lady Caroline. 'I have just recalled a luncheon appointment.'

Violet was delighted when she saw her friend marching purposefully across the restaurant of the Café de Paris. The last two days had been dreadful. Everywhere they went, the Duchamps insisted on coming with them. Worse, Henri had forbidden Violet from bringing Toto along, since the little poodle tried to bite his ankles whenever he saw him.

Once or twice, Violet had tactfully suggested that they give the Duchamps some time to themselves and take a trip out to Lady Caroline's villa, but that didn't work either. Florence always managed to find a reason to keep them in Monte Carlo. The last time she had insisted on a tour of the aquarium, even though all of them had seen it twice before. It was almost as if they didn't want to let Violet and Garth out of their sight. Moreover, their conversation was extremely boring. All they wanted to talk about was Lord and Lady Winters' friendship with Count and Countess Drakensburg and who else they knew in Monte Carlo. Indeed, their persistence was almost distasteful.

Now Violet practically jumped out of her chair as Lady Caroline appeared at her side. 'How *lovely* to see you,' she cried, and kissed her firmly on the cheek.

The old lady took Violet's hand and kissed her in return. Now she was sure she had made the right decision. The girl's relief at seeing her could not be mistaken.

'May I introduce you to Garth Hudson, my father's ward?' said Violet, knowing perfectly well that the Duchamps would be offended that she had not introduced them first.

The implication of Violet's decision was not lost on Lady Caroline and she grew more determined than ever to find out what was going on. Garth stood up and shook her hand.

'I am delighted to meet you at last,' he said. 'Violet has told me so much about Le Soleil.'

'Then you must visit as soon as possible,' said Lady Caroline pointedly. She smiled at Garth and he smiled back, aware that they were all playing parts in an increasingly uncomfortable game.

'And this is Monsieur and Madame Duchamps,' said Violet, without further introduction.

Lady Caroline held Violet's eye for a split second. Then she bowed distantly and offered her hand first to Florence and then to Henri.

Henri Duchamps bowed back, but his sharp face was pinched and he couldn't hide his annoyance. Everyone knew that this was the moment when he should ask Lady Caroline to join them but he said nothing. It was clear that neither he nor his wife was at all pleased by her unexpected appearance.

Violet felt her heart banging with fury. How dare this man behave like a bounder? Over the past two days and for the first time in her life, Violet had begun to question her father's judgement and it made her feel extremely uncomfortable. How *could* he have

131

agreed to leave her and Garth in the care of such dreadful people? At first she had put it down to her parents' hurried departure and the need to make arrangements quickly, but that still didn't make sense. There must be another reason. But for the life of her, Violet couldn't work out what it was and, in the meantime, she and Garth had been forced to put up with the French couple's prying, unpleasant company. Suddenly Violet didn't care how much she offended the Duchamps.

'We would be delighted if you would join us for lunch, Lady Caroline,' she said.

Florence Duchamps flushed and shot a glance at her husband.

'Why, of course, we would be honoured, Your Ladyship,' said Henri in a thin voice. Garth held up his hand for an extra chair to be brought to the table.

'How very kind of you, Garth,' said Lady Caroline. She turned to Henri Duchamps and said pointedly, 'Thank you, Monsieur, for your charming invitation.'

A chair appeared and Lady Caroline sat down firmly between Violet and Florence Duchamps. 'I came to thank your dear mother for her kind gift, only to discover they are away. How lucky that I bumped into you.' She touched Violet's hand. 'I am quite put out that you have not brought Garth to see me.'

'We could come tomorrow,' replied Violet quickly. 'Would that be convenient?'

Henri Duchamps coughed. 'Have you forgotten we are visiting the aquarium in the morning, Violet? And in the afternoon—'

'The *aquarium*?' cried Lady Caroline in disbelief. 'That ghastly collection of dirty fish tanks?'

Violet looked into Henri Duchamps's weasel face and said sweetly, 'Have you forgotten, Monsieur, that we have visited the aquarium twice already?'

The awkward silence was broken by the appearance of a waiter.

'*Mesdames et messieurs.*' A seal-like young man in black and white bowed to them all.

'Today the café pays tribute to the casino.' He bowed. 'All luncheon dishes are either red or black.'

Violet turned to Lady Caroline. 'We were just talking of Count and Countess Drakensburg,' she said smoothly. 'Madame Duchamps was asking after the Count. He won a fortune on red the other night.'

'Did he, by God?' cried Lady Caroline. 'Well, bully for him!'

She picked up her menu and spoke to the waiter who was standing at her side. 'In his honour, I shall have the prawns and salmon with a beetroot salad, followed by a strawberry mousse, please.'

'The same for me, please.' Violet put down her menu and smiled at Henri Duchamps. 'Do you have any interest in gambling, Monsieur?'

Henri Duchamps returned her smile but his eyes were hard. 'None at all,' he said shortly. 'However, I shall play a black hand to your red.' He picked up his own menu and turned to the waiter. 'Caviar, jugged hare and chocolate profiteroles.'

You're a filthy liar! thought Violet to herself, fighting to keep the anger from her face. She paused before saying in a persistent voice, 'Then do tell me, Monsieur, why would you want to come to Monte Carlo, where there is practically nothing to do *but* gamble?' The words hung in the air like a challenge.

'To enjoy the benefit of the climate,' replied Henri Duchamps. He stared coldly at Violet. 'Perhaps you have forgotten our terrible upset in Paris?'

Now Violet felt her face go red and, seeing what had happened, Garth diverted Henri Duchamps's attention to himself. 'Since you have referred to the dreadful robbery,' he said smoothly, 'I was wondering if the culprit had been apprehended?'

'Sadly, my wife's jewellery has not yet been returned.' Henri Duchamps paused. 'And I understand Mrs Stuyvesant Fish is in the same position.'

'Dear Ladyship!' shrieked a familiar voice. 'What happiness! What joy!' Marie Cherkassky barrelled across the restaurant floor and grabbed Lady Caroline's hand. 'And here also my two greatest friends from England and America!'

Violet stood up and kissed Marie warmly on her cheeks. She couldn't have been more pleased to see anyone. Now at least the icily awkward atmosphere would be replaced by Marie's noisiness.

'Why, Marie!' said Lady Caroline. 'I do hope you are not deserting your piano for the gambling table.' She turned to Henri and Florence. 'May I introduce Marie Cherkassky? She plays the piano quite beautifully.'

Marie dragged a chair from the next table and sat down. 'You are very kind, Your Ladyship.' She turned to Florence and Henri Duchamps and beamed at them. 'Yes, I am beautiful genius. It is true.'

A team of waiters arrived and set down the first courses and a ragged pattern of red and black emerged on the table.

Before Marie could demand an explanation, Garth told her that the café was paying tribute to the casino. Then, suddenly, he decided to provoke her, just to see how the Duchamps would react. 'We were just speaking of Count and Countess Drakensburg—' he began.

'Poof!' snorted Marie furiously. 'What do I care for those fakes!'

There was a *crunch* of breaking glass. The thin goblet Florence Duchamps had been holding in her clenched fingers shattered into tiny pieces and clattered on her plate.

'Forgive me, Madame,' cried Marie. She slapped her hand on her chest. 'Can it be that these fakes is friends to you?'

'Marie!' cried Lady Caroline sternly.

But Marie wasn't listening. 'Please, Madame!' She grabbed Florence Duchamps's wrists. 'I beg of you. Do not trust these peoples. They are –' she paused, hunting for the right words – 'they are the bad sort.'

Florence Duchamps stared at Marie as if she was

looking at a ghost. 'You must excuse me, Your Ladyship,' she said in a faltering voice. She stared hopelessly at her husband. 'Henri, I fear I am not . . . very . . . well.'

For a moment, no one spoke. Even Lady Caroline was taken aback. 'My cab is outside,' she said. 'It is at your disposal.'

'Thank you, Lady Caroline,' said Henri stiffly. He stepped over to his wife and helped her to her feet. 'But our hotel is only a short walk away. I shall leave Violet in your care.' Without waiting for a reply, he led his wife from the room.

'I think you should all apologise,' said Lady Caroline when the Duchamps had left. 'Especially you, Marie. Your behaviour was totally unacceptable. In fact I think you ought to go home right now and write them a letter.'

Marie opened her mouth to object but took one look at Lady Caroline and closed it again. She stood up and bowed to Violet and Garth. 'I am sorry,' she said. 'My mouth is too big for my stomach.' She stared at them with sad eyes. 'It is not the first time I have this problem.'

Violet looked at Marie's crumpled face. She was

almost in tears. She stood up and squeezed her hand. 'Don't worry,' Violet whispered. 'Let's meet up again soon.'

Marie nodded, raised her hand to say goodbye and shuffled miserably out of the room.

For a moment no one spoke, then Lady Caroline looked up at Garth and Violet. 'That incident was most unfortunate,' she said in a worried voice. 'Marie Cherkassky is remarkably talented and indeed much cleverer than you might believe. However, her manners are quite dreadful. And even though I can understand why you dislike the Duchamps, Violet, you really *must* be more tactful. They could make your lives very unpleasant while your parents are away.' She shook her head. 'Have you any idea why your father would leave you with such ghastly people?'

Lady Caroline listened in silence as Violet explained how Florence Duchamps had reported seeing Madame Poisson in the casino and how her mother had wanted to sack her. 'So they agreed to send her away for a week and that the Duchamps would be our guardians.'

'I don't understand it at all,' replied Lady Caroline. 'Your father knows perfectly well that Madame

Poisson is an excellent card player and enjoys an evening at the casino.'

'Then why all this fuss about sending her to Paris for a week?' asked Violet.

'I have no idea,' said Lady Caroline. 'I can only think that he has some plan in mind. Either that or his judgement has gone soft in the sun.'

Violet looked away.

'I'm sorry, my dear,' said Lady Caroline. 'That was rude of me.'

'Not all,' replied Violet. 'It's exactly what I was thinking myself.'

Garth was practically squirming in his seat. 'Excuse me, Your Ladyship, but I think we should make our apologies to the Duchamps as soon as possible. If we hurry now, we'll catch up with them.'

'Yes, do go.' The old lady looked at the plates of uneaten red and black *hors d'oeuvres*. 'I'll sort things out here.' She stood up and kissed Violet goodbye. 'And remember, my dear, if you have any problems, come straight to me.'

Five minutes later, Garth and Violet were threading their way through the crowds on the promenade.

Violet looked around. 'We'll never find them,' she said. 'And anyway, if you think I'm apologizing—'

'Of course I don't,' said Garth. 'I just wanted get out of that restaurant.'

'So where are we going?'

'To the Riviera Palace Hotel. I want to ask the porter there a couple of questions.'

Everything at the Riviera Palace Hotel was pink and white, and that included the porter's uniform. As agreed, Violet smiled prettily while Garth chatted to a young man whose carrot-orange hair and freckled face clashed horribly with the colour of his cap and jacket.

'We're supposed to be looking for friends of our parents,' said Garth, rolling his eyes. 'Well, delivering a message really.'

The porter smiled. He liked Americans. They were always much more friendly than the English, who treated you like some kind of peasant. And they always gave bigger tips.

'What's the name?' asked the porter. 'Have they just arrived?'

Garth shook his head. 'No, they've been here for a

few days. It's Monsieur and Madame Duchamps.'

The porter frowned. He hadn't seen that name on any of the lists. Nor did he remember hearing it. 'Hold on a minute,' he said. 'I'll just check with the manager.' He paused and looked at Garth in a meaningful way. 'But he's kind of old-fashioned about this sort of thing.'

'That's fine.' Garth smiled and handed over a one-hundred-franc note from his monthly allowance.

The porter smiled back and put the note in his pocket.

Half an hour later, Violet and Garth walked in stunned silence along the seafront.

'Maybe the porter was lying,' said Violet at last.

'Why would he lie?' replied Garth. 'The fact is, no one by the name of Duchamps has ever stayed at that hotel.'

'Maybe they said they were staying there to look smart in front of my parents,' said Violet. She thought for a moment. 'I think they're mixed up with the Count and Countess somehow. Both of them seem to be out to impress. But that doesn't make them thieves.'

'Quite right,' said Garth, a grin suddenly spreading across his face. 'So I think it's about time we found out.'

Violet followed his gaze and her heart jumped in her chest.

Count and Countess Drakensburg were sitting in a cab which was turning into the Hermitage!

TEN

'There's an urgent letter for you and Monsieur 'Udson, Lady Violet,' said the hotel manager, as Garth and Violet came in through the garden door.

He reached under his desk and handed over a white envelope. 'This is Mrs Stuyvesant Fish's writing!' cried Violet. She looked into Garth's face and saw the same excitement she was feeling herself. 'It's about the jewel thieves, I know it!'

'Come on,' said Garth, hurrying her out of the hallway. 'The last thing we want to do now is bump into the Drakensburgs.'

'How about some tea and detective work on my balcony?'

'Sounds good to me!'

*

Five minutes later, Violet handed the letter over to Garth. 'Read it aloud,' she said firmly. 'Maybe it will help us work this out.'

'*Dear Violet,*' read Garth. '*I am writing in haste concerning a very serious matter which has to do with the theft of my jewellery in Paris. I understand your parents are away in Italy, therefore I must put my trust in you and Garth. The* gendarmes *in Paris are now sure that these thefts are the work of criminals disguising themselves as guests or members of high society. Unfortunately they still have no idea of the criminals' identity. Two events have now taken place that are causing me great worry. I have learned from your father of the theft of your mother's jewellery. I have also just been informed by my dear friends the Baron and Baroness Orzo that they are arriving at the Hermitage in Monte Carlo in two days' time. I have spoken to them of my worries but I cannot convince the Baroness to leave her diamonds in a bank vault in Paris. I am now asking if you and Garth would be kind enough to keep an eye on this situation until your parents return. Since you are staying in the same hotel, there is a possibility that you might notice something suspicious and possibly prevent what would be a catastrophe. I am*

144

aware that Monsieur and Madame Duchamps are now staying at the Hermitage, along with Count and Countess Drakensburg, but as they are not acquainted with the Baron and Baroness and since I know neither of them, I do not feel I can share my concerns with them.

With much affection,
Gwendoline Stuyvesant Fish.
P.S. I trust Toto is thriving in the sea air.'

Violet put three lumps of sugar in Garth's cup and poured him tea from a pretty white-and-yellow teapot. 'So, the Duchamps are staying here too. Maybe that's why the porter at the Riviera Palace didn't know them! We've *got* to figure out what is going on before the Baron and Baroness arrive.'

Garth nodded. 'I'm sure now that the thefts are an inside job.' He picked up an almond biscuit and chewed it thoughtfully. 'And the fact is, it's got to be the Duchamps or the Drakensburgs. One or other of them has been present at every robbery.'

Violet sipped at her own tea and tried to organise her thoughts. 'Do you know, I think Father suspects the Duchamps and that's why he left us with them.'

145

Garth frowned. 'I don't understand.'

'I'm not positive I do, either, but it suddenly occurred to me that if the Duchamps think he trusts them, then they might also think they've got away with it and may do something incriminating as a result.'

'But the Duchamps weren't here when your mother's jewellery was stolen. It was the Drakensburgs. And it was the Countess who was so keen to keep Mrs Stuyvesant Fish in Paris.'

Violet put down her cup. 'I wonder if both couples are in it together.'

But Garth wasn't listening. 'Remember when we first saw the Duchamps on the boulevard and I thought I heard them planning to steal a diamond necklace?'

Violet nodded. 'Do you think you were right all along?'

'Maybe,' said Garth. Then he shook his head. 'No, that idea doesn't work, because they'd already left when Mrs Stuyvesant Fish was robbed.'

'They could have seen her wearing the jewellery while they were at the hotel and decided to come back and steal it,' said Violet. 'The same applies to my mother. Maybe they saw her ring and the diamond necklace and decided to follow us down south.' She frowned. 'Then again, as you say, they had already left the hotel when my mother was robbed.'

'That doesn't mean they weren't around,' replied Garth. He slurped a mouthful of tea and surreptitiously stirred in a fourth lump of sugar. 'I think the Duchamps *are* the thieves, Vi. I think they faked their robbery at the Ritz to throw the *gendarmes* off their trail.'

'No, I disagree,' said Violet. 'You're forgetting that first dinner at the Ritz when the Drakensburgs arrived with Grand Duke Michael. I was sitting opposite the Countess and I'll never forget the look on her face when she found out Mrs Stuyvesant Fish had changed her plans and was coming with us to Monte Carlo. So it's pretty strange that Mrs Stuyvesant Fish is robbed that night and then here they disappear after my mother is robbed.'

'But they've come back,' said Garth. 'If they were the thieves, why would they do that? Besides, the Count won a fortune at the casino the other night.'

'Don't forget what Marie said about them being fakes.'

'Marie's crazy.'

'Lady Caroline doesn't think so. No manners, but not crazy.' Violet stared at Garth. 'And why would Madame Duchamps be so taken aback that she crushes a glass in her hand?' Violet shook her head. 'Maybe you're right. Maybe the Duchamps *are* the thieves. After all, we know now that they never stayed at the Riviera Palace.'

Garth picked up Mrs Stuyvesant Fish's letter. 'So what do we do about the Baron and Baroness Orzo?'

Violet looked at her tea. It would be cold now. She ate a sugar lump instead. 'Maybe we should tell Frank Winalot what we know.'

'The problem is, all we've got are suspicions,' said Garth. 'And if we say something now, we could scare the real thieves away. Then we'd *never* get your mother's jewellery back.'

Violet stared at Garth. She knew him so well, sometimes she could read his mind. 'So you're suggesting we use the Baroness's diamonds as bait?'

'Have you got a better idea?'

There was a tap on the door.

Garth got up and opened it.

'Monsieur 'Udson?'

'*Oui?*'

'*C'est pour vous et Mademoiselle Violette.*' The valet bowed and put an envelope into Garth's hand.

'It's from Marie,' said Garth, turning the envelope over. A wax seal was imprinted with the letters MC.

'What does she say?'

Garth ripped open the envelope and pulled out a single sheet of paper covered in big curly writing. 'She wants to meet us in the gardens outside the casino at six. She has something important to tell us.'

Violet looked at her watch. It was half-past five. 'If we leave now, we'll just get there in time.' She whistled for Toto and clipped on his lead.

'And if we see the Duchamps?' said Garth, pulling on his jacket.

'We'll smile and be polite,' replied Violet as she fastened her cape around her shoulders. 'We're good at that.'

The sun was sinking below the horizon and turning the sea gold as Toto pulled Violet and Garth down the promenade and into the gardens around the casino. Violet looked up at the balustrade wall beyond the entrance. It was from there that she had seen Henri

Duchamps walking through the main doors the night the Count had won his fortune. Now her eye travelled down from the balcony and into the gardens below.

She stopped in her tracks and gripped Garth's arm.

'What's the matter?' asked Garth. 'Have you seen Marie?'

Violet shook her head and pointed into the garden. It was laid out with chairs and tables, each in their own pool of light from tall wrought-iron lamps. Men and woman were drinking and talking and the light from the lamps gave the garden the atmosphere of a carnival.

The Duchamps were sitting with a group of people at one of the tables. Florence's short blonde hair shone almost white under the lamplight. She looked completely at ease, leaning back in her chair and sipping her early evening cocktail. It was impossible to believe that this was the same woman who had staggered, distraught, out of the restaurant on her husband's arm only that lunchtime.

Violet shivered. She still couldn't be sure whether it was the Duchamps or the Drakensburgs who were behind the robberies but it had to be one of them and the very sight of the Duchamps made her feel sick.

'Violet! Stop daydreaming!' Garth pulled her by the arm. 'Let's try and hear what they're saying.' They ducked in and out of the shadows until they could hide behind a thick bush not far from the Duchamps' table.

Suddenly one of the people at the table, who Violet didn't recognise, jumped up and ran over to a short, bald man and a plump woman in a striped travelling outfit who were crossing towards them. 'Baron Orzo! Baroness! How delightful! We weren't expecting you until tomorrow!'

Henri Duchamps' head jerked around, while Florence sat back in her chair and finished her cocktail. But Violet saw her eyes move to the new-comers and settle on them.

The short man bowed. 'Lady Yarmouth. What a joy to see you! Yes indeed, we left Paris early.' He placed a gloved hand on his wife's arm. 'My dear Sophy was too impatient for the card table!'

There was a ripple of laughter. As Lady Yarmouth made the introductions, it was clear the Duchamps were the only members of the party who had not met the Baron or his wife before.

Violet watched as Florence Duchamps slid over

and began to talk to the Baroness. She seemed to hang on every word the older woman said. In return, the Baroness seemed to take to her and, sure enough, the two of them were soon in animated conversation.

You fraud, thought Violet. It was the same trick Florence Duchamps had used on her mother in the saloon car on the way down to Monte Carlo.

Violet felt her cheeks flush with anger. Florence Duchamps might be good enough to fool her mother, but she wasn't fooling *her*.

She bent down to pick up Toto to be sure he didn't run off. In the dusky light, she didn't see the cactus in the flower bed. Its sharp spines went straight into her hand and she dropped the puppy with a yelp of pain.

The next moment, Toto ran across the grass and bit Henri Duchamps on the ankle.

'Oh, no,' whispered Violet, rubbing at her sore hand. '*Now* what are we going to do?'

'Bluff it out,' said Garth. 'Come on.' He took her arm and they walked into the light.

'Lady Violet?' The Baron stood up as Violet and Garth appeared out of the bushes.

Before Violet could reply, Toto tore a piece off Henri Duchamps' trousers.

'I'm so sorry, Monsieur,' cried Violet. It seemed she was talking to both men at the same time as she grabbed Toto and clipped on his lead. 'He doesn't usually—'

'I don't care *what* he usually does,' snarled Henri Duchamps. 'That dog is a menace!'

The Baron roared with laughter. 'It seems he feels the same way about you, Monsieur!'

Laughter rippled around the table and Garth watched Henri Duchamps bite his lip, fighting to control the fury darkening his face.

'Allow me to introduce myself,' cried the Baron to Violet. 'Baron Gustav Orzo.' He grasped Violet's hand and smiled at her, his eyes shining with humour in his round, pudgy face. 'I must say, your photograph in London barely does you justice.'

'My photograph?' blurted Violet.

'On your father's desk. He said it was a recent portrait.'

'I had no idea you knew my father,' said Violet. 'I'm sorry, Monsieur.'

'Really, Gustav,' cried the Baroness, turning from Florence Duchamps, whose interested expression had turned into a cold scowl. 'You mustn't tease the poor girl!' She took Violet's hand and smiled. 'I am

Baroness Sophy. And you must be Lord Percy's ward,' she said to Garth.

'Of course,' cried the Baron, grasping Garth's hand after his wife. 'Young Garth Hudson. I am delighted to meet you.'

'Do join us,' said Lady Yarmouth. 'I'm a great friend of Caroline Egmont and she has spoken so highly of you both.' She looked down at the puppy, who was squirming in Violet's arms. 'And what is this little devil's name?'

'Toto.' Violet turned again to Henri Duchamps. 'I must apologise again, Monsieur.'

'No damage.' Henri Duchamps managed a thin-lipped smile. 'I am honoured your dog has such good taste.'

'We travelled down with Violet's parents,' announced Florence Duchamps, smoothly establishing their credentials. She smiled. 'Little Toto was quite taken by Henri on the train.'

'You mean the puppy bit him then, too?' asked Lady Yarmouth.

Florence Duchamps nodded as more laughter went round the table. It was clear her husband was not amused by her remark, however.

The Baron looked at Florence Duchamps more closely. 'I had no idea you were acquainted with Lord Percy and Lady Eleanor,' he said pleasantly.

'Oh, we are very good friends,' declared Florence.

'Indeed, yes!' added Henri Duchamps. He stepped across to Violet's side and went to put his hand on her shoulder. 'We are acting as Violet and Garth's guardians while her parents are in Italy.'

'What a responsibility!' said the Baron, watching as Violet moved sideways before Henri Duchamps could touch her. 'I must say I wouldn't have a clue how to entertain such a pair of enquiring young minds.'

Suddenly Garth remembered Marie. With the shock of the unexpected confrontation with the Duchamps and the arrival of the Baron and Baroness, he had forgotten all about her.

Violet turned, sensing Garth's restlessness, and found herself looking across the gardens to the front entrance of the casino. Her eyes nearly popped out of her head!

Madame Poisson was walking through the main doors, arm in arm with a complete stranger, and grinning from ear to ear!

'Please excuse us,' cried Violet. She turned to the

Baron and away from Henri Duchamps. 'Toto needs his supper. Goodbye!'

Henri Duchamps stiffened and was about to speak before he caught a warning glance from his wife and changed his mind. By that time, Violet was halfway across the garden and heading towards the promenade.

'Violet,' cried Garth, catching up with her, 'what are you doing? We're supposed to meet Marie!'

Violet turned as she ran down the steps. 'I just saw the codfish coming out of the casino! If we hurry, we'll catch her!'

'But she's in Paris,' said Garth as they both ran along the promenade.

'That's what I was *told*,' replied Violet. 'Garth! She was grinning from ear to ear. She looked as if she'd won a fortune!'

But it was as if Madame Poisson didn't want to be found. Though Garth and Violet ran up every little street, somehow the codfish had completely disappeared.

'Rats!' muttered Garth after they had searched every cul-de-sac and alley. 'Now we've lost out twice.'

'I don't think Marie ever showed up,' replied

Violet. 'If she'd been hiding in the garden, she would have found us on the street.' She bent down and picked up Toto, who was tired and beginning to drag on his lead. 'It's all getting too confusing.'

'It's more than confusing,' said Garth. 'It could be dangerous. If the Duchamps really *are* the thieves, they must be suspicious of us by now and they won't want us spoiling their plans for getting hold of the Baroness's diamonds.'

'You're right,' said Violet at last. 'I think we should talk to Frank and Lily.'

But when they asked for Mr and Mrs Winalot at the hotel, they were told the Americans had left to cruise around the bay on their yacht.

'*Mais il y a quelque chose pour vous.*' The manager handed Garth a small, beautifully wrapped box and gave Violet an envelope with the Drakensburg crest on the back.

Inside the box was a model of Frank's motor yacht and an invitation to a party the following night. Garth held out a note. 'They want to pick us up tomorrow morning for a sail around the bay.'

'That's the best news we've had all day,' said Violet as she opened the letter. 'Hmm, this is not so good.

The Countess is asking us to join her for coffee.' Violet looked at Garth. 'I don't want to see her.'

'Nor do I,' replied Garth. 'I think we should stay in our rooms until we leave. That way, we'll be out of here before the Duchamps have woken up. And we won't have to face the Count and Countess, either.'

'But what happens if they've both been invited to Frank's party, too?'

'Safety in numbers,' replied Garth, as they walked along the passage to Violet's room. 'Just lock your door tonight.'

'This is crazy,' said Violet. 'We should get out of here altogether. Why don't we stay with Lady Caroline until my parents get back?'

'Good idea. I'll leave a note with the *concierge* to send on our luggage first thing tomorrow morning.'

Violet nodded. 'Do you think I can bring Toto on the yacht?'

'Of course you can,' replied Garth. He paused. 'Don't forget to lock your door.'

'I won't.'

That night Violet lay in bed, listening to the surf rattling the pebbles. With each surge of the sea,

she changed her mind about who was responsible for the robberies. First it was the Duchamps. Then it was the Count and Countess.

Then Madame Poisson's grinning face filled her mind. It was more than a grin. Her codfish had looked as if she was going to explode with delight. Violet remembered what Lady Caroline had said about her governess's skills at the gambling table and suddenly she was sure that Madame Poisson had not been sent to Paris, as her father had said, but had been in Monte Carlo all along.

But why was her father making up such lies? If he had wanted her and Garth to watch what the Duchamps were up to, why hadn't he told her the truth? It wasn't as if they hadn't joined forces before to solve mysteries. What was so different this time that he couldn't trust her?

Toto whined beside her and turned over. Violet held him close to her chest and fell into a troubled sleep.

ELEVEN

Frank Winalot's yacht was a floating palace. Grand, sweeping staircases led to gilded saloons full of antique French furniture. Everywhere, elaborate mirrors hung from the walls and Turkish rugs were scattered on the polished mahogany floors.

'She's got eight hundred electric light bulbs,' boasted Frank, as pleased with his boat as a child with a new toy. 'And a machine that makes twelve hundred pounds of ice every day.' He handed them each a tall glass of lemonade, filled to the top with star-shaped ice cubes.

'And you won't *believe* my bedroom, Violet!' said Lily. 'It's as big as a room at the Ritz.' She smiled at her husband. 'And twice as pretty.'

'I don't know why we stay in a hotel at all,' said Frank, swallowing his lemonade in one gulp and pouring out another.

Lily sat down on a padded deck chair and indicated for Garth and Violet to sit in the empty chairs on either side. 'So, what's going on ashore?'

Garth and Violet sat down and looked at each other. This was the moment to tell Frank and Lily what they knew, and what they suspected, and what they couldn't understand. But neither of them knew where to begin.

'Goodness gracious!' cried Lily. 'Such long faces!'

'More lemonade,' cried Frank, ringing a small bell by his side. He patted Violet's arm and smiled. 'Talking is thirsty work and I have a feeling we've got lots to talk about.'

The morning came and went and the four of them were still talking. White-coated stewards served lunch on deck under a striped blue-and-white awning. It was Frank's favourite – steak sandwiches, corn relish, ketchup and fried potatoes. Violet and Garth loved the change from the fussy French food they had been eating since they arrived and, for a moment, it was almost like being back in New York.

'So you think the Duchamps are behind the robberies?' said Frank to Garth at last.

Garth nodded. But even as he explained his reasons, it occurred to him that perhaps the Count and Countess were using the Duchamps as stooges.

Frank turned to Violet. 'And *you* think it's the Count and Countess?'

'I don't know any more,' said Violet. 'But I'm almost positive my parents' visit to Italy was not a spur of the moment decision. I think they left us with the Duchamps to try and trick them into making a mistake.' She shrugged. 'And so far they haven't. Now all we can think of doing is using the Baroness's diamonds as bait.'

Violet turned to Lily. 'Madame Duchamps was certainly playing the same game with the Baroness as she did with my mother on the train.'

Lily nodded. 'And you're sure it was your governess you saw outside the casino?'

'Positive,' said Violet. 'Absolutely positive.'

Frank leaned back against the back of his padded chair. Beyond the polished mahogany deck railings, across a turquoise sea, the buildings of Monte Carlo sparkled white against the limestone cliffs. 'I think it's time I did a little explaining,' he said. He waited until the remains of the four chocolate and vanilla ice cream sundaes had been cleared away. Then he took a deep breath and began to speak.

For the next hour, Garth and Violet were silent. It turned out that Frank was a secret and unofficial member of a private international detection agency that specialised in serious jewellery thefts. He had the perfect cover as a millionaire playboy. When the Duchamps and Mrs Stuyvesant Fish were robbed in Paris, these were the latest in a string of thefts that had recently taken place in capitals throughout Europe. But all that had been established was that the thefts seemed to be the work of insiders. There was still no clue as to who they were. As soon as Frank and Lily had met Lady Eleanor, it was clear to them that she was likely to be a target for the thieves.

'I warned your father,' said Frank to Violet, 'but he offered to help instead. And to tell you the truth, I was delighted.' Frank smiled ruefully. 'I'm sure you all know what a reputation your father has for, uh, solving problems. And not just him, you two do as well. So I agreed immediately. It was the first lucky break I'd had on this case. Just like you, we had our suspicions, but no proof.'

Garth leaned forward. 'Have the Duchamps and the Count and Countess always been suspected?'

Frank shook his head. 'No, there were a number of different people involved, but we could never get a proper lead on them before they disappeared. Then the Duchamps and the Count and Countess turned up in Paris, and it seemed to me that a pattern was emerging. There was the occasional robbery but nothing to attract suspicion. Both couples seem extremely well connected but, as you know, there is something not quite right about both of them.'

'So if my father knew what was going on,' asked Violet, 'was the jewellery that was stolen from my mother fake?'

Frank shook his head. 'Your mother ordered paste replicas as soon as she knew of the danger, but they arrived here a day late and she took the risk of wearing her own diamonds that one night.' He paused. 'You can imagine how she blames herself.'

Violet could barely believe what she was hearing.

'You mean my mother was only *pretending* to be friends with Florence Duchamps and the Countess?'

Frank nodded. 'An impressive performance, wouldn't you say?' Then his face went serious. 'The problem is that, so far, we still haven't caught them red-handed. And in the past, as I said, the thieves disappeared. Your father was unsure about the decision to leave you in the care of the Duchamps, but when they tried to ingratiate themselves by reporting Madame Poisson's presence in the casino, he decided to use that as the reason for asking them to look after you. It was the best he could do to keep them in Monte Carlo.'

'And tonight, as you worked out for yourselves, the Baron has agreed to use his wife's diamonds as bait,' said Lily. 'It's our last chance to flush out the real culprits.'

Violet thought of the Baron's mention of her photograph in London. 'Did the Baron agree to help to return a favour to my father?' she asked.

Frank raised his eyebrows in surprise. 'Yes, as it happens, he did.'

Violet nodded. She was too discreet to ask what the original favour had been. Her father's professional life was a mystery and she knew she would have to leave it at that.

'Have both the Duchamps and the Count and Countess been invited to your party tonight?' asked Garth.

'Of course,' replied Frank.

'So it's a showdown,' said Violet. 'How *exciting*!'

'Are the *gendarmes* involved, too?' asked Garth.

'To an extent,' replied Frank. 'But they know nothing of what I've just told you. Money talks and thieves always have friends in the police.'

At that moment a member of the crew, dressed immaculately in white and wearing a sailor's hat, came up with a note in his hand. Frank opened it and whistled thoughtfully through his teeth. 'No Duchamps. They send their compliments but regret they have a previous engagement. Pity. I thought the Baroness's diamonds would be irresistible.'

'Especially since they've already met her,' said Violet. 'And Florence Duchamps has already done her groundwork.'

'Maybe that's the reason they're not coming,' said Frank thoughtfully. 'They don't need me any more to make the introduction.'

Garth turned to Violet. 'What if the Duchamps and the Drakensburgs find out we've left the hotel? It's not going to look good.'

'I particularly asked the *concierge* to say nothing to anyone,' said Violet, staring at her hands. 'Except Madame Poisson or my parents.'

'Porters can be bribed,' said Frank in a low voice. 'You must both be very careful.'

'How do I look?' asked Violet as she and Garth walked along the yacht's wide panelled corridor towards the main drawing room. The sound of people talking was like a field full of crows cawing.

'Utterly charming,' said Garth, in his terrible English accent.

Violet looked at him. Without her mother telling her what to wear, she had chosen a loose cream lawn dress with a gauzy yellow overskirt and a light turquoise silk jacket. It was more informal than usual for the evening but tonight Violet had decided to be comfortable.

'Are you teasing me?' she asked Garth.

'Certainly not,' replied Garth, who was wearing full evening dress with a stiff white collar. 'You look comfortable and I'm jealous.' He poked the lumpy satin bag she was holding. 'But why are you carrying that around?'

There was a muffled *yap* and Toto's head appeared out of the bag. He looked at Garth as fiercely as he could manage, then ducked back inside again.

Garth rolled his eyes. 'Let me guess. You want to polish his social skills?'

'Something like that.'

They were laughing as they walked into the crowded room. Even though she had known the Countess would be there, the sight of her talking to Lady Yarmouth made Violet shiver. The tall, red-headed woman had the predatory look of a hawk.

'Violet!' Garth touched her arm. 'Pull yourself together! We're going to have to speak to them sooner or later. If they suspect anything, we'll let everyone down.'

'I'll do my best,' said Violet, 'but she really gives me the creeps.'

'Violet,' cried a voice behind her.

Violet turned, and as she looked into the Baroness's bright eyes she made herself smile.

'I was hoping to have news of your dear mother.'

The Baroness paused. 'Are you quite well, my dear? You look pale.'

'I'm perfectly well, thank you,' replied Violet, although her throat felt so tight she could barely swallow. 'Perhaps I had too much sun this afternoon.'

'Dreadful star, the sun,' said the Baroness, placing a soft white hand on Violet's arm. 'Really, you should carry a parasol and wear a broad-brimmed hat at all times.'

But Violet wasn't listening. Instead she was staring at the Baroness's neck. She was wearing a beautiful eight-string choker of black pearls attached to an oval diamond the size of a gull's egg. It seemed to be the only thing that stopped the Baroness's chin from meeting her chest. 'What a beautiful necklace,' Violet said.

'My grandmother's,' said the Baroness in a matter-of-fact voice. 'It was made in St Petersburg, for the coronation of Alexander III. But let's not talk about jewellery. How is your mother? Mrs Stuyvesant Fish told me everything.'

Violet looked into the Baroness's kind, friendly eyes and wondered if she knew that her diamond necklace was being used as bait. In the end she decided she didn't. She was about to reply when she smelled the scent of jasmine and the next moment Countess Drakensburg was standing beside them. It was clear that she wanted to meet the Baroness, but though Violet knew it would seem odd for her not to make the necessary introductions, somehow she couldn't do it.

'Violet, my dear,' said the Countess in her thin, brittle voice. 'I'm so sorry you couldn't join us for coffee this morning.' And without waiting for an answer, she turned to the Baroness. 'Allow me to introduce myself. I am Countess Drakensburg.' She held out a hand that sparkled with rings. 'I overheard you speak of Mrs Stuyvesant Fish,' she said with her wolf-like smile. 'She is a great friend of ours. We met her in Paris with dear Violet's mother and father.'

Baroness Orzo held the Countess's hand for the shortest time, then let it go. It was clear to Violet that she didn't like the look of this red-haired woman whose dark complexion was at odds with her pale eyes.

'Speaking of Lord Percy and Lady Eleanor,' continued the Countess, 'we had hoped to see them on our return from Vienna. Are they travelling else-where?'

Violet stared as closely as she dared at the Countess's face. She seemed genuinely surprised at her parents' absence.

'Surely you must have heard of poor Eleanor's robbery?' asked the Baroness.

'The Count and Countess had gone before my mother discovered the loss of her jewels,' said Violet, positive now that the Baroness had no idea of what was really going on. She turned back to the Countess. 'They are in Italy, Countess. My mother was extremely upset at the loss of her engagement ring. My father thought it best they went away. She tried to send word to you to cancel your visit to Grasse but you were not to be found.'

The Countess stared first at the Baroness and then at Violet, apparently in utter confusion. 'I'm so sorry,' she gasped. 'How dreadful! I had no idea a robbery had taken place! The Count was called unexpectedly to Vienna and we were obliged to take the early train.' She turned to Violet. 'I left your mother a note with the *concierge* but I see from your face that it was never delivered.' She opened her a sequined evening purse and pressed a jasmine-scented handkerchief to her nose as if she was about to burst into tears. 'How absolutely appalling!'

'My dear Countess,' said Baroness Orzo, 'calm yourself, for heaven's sake. You are upsetting the poor girl.'

'I'm sorry, my dear,' cried the Countess. 'If only I'd known! But when I didn't see you this morning and asked for you, the *concierge* told me you had just left to stay with Lady Caroline and I presumed . . .'

Violet felt her head begin to spin. Had the Countess bribed the *concierge* to find out that she and Garth had left the hotel? For the first time, Violet understood that both she and Garth could be in real danger.

From the other side of the room, Garth saw Violet's face turn the same colour as her dress and quickly crossed over to her. 'Violet,' he said lightly, 'Lady Yarmouth would love to have a word with you.' He turned and smiled at the Countess. 'Do please excuse us.' Then he led Violet quickly away.

'What is it, Vi?' he asked when they couldn't be overheard. 'What's wrong?'

'She knows we've left the hotel,' replied Violet. She

looked into Garth's face. 'But I don't think it's the Drakensburgs any more. She had no idea my mother had been robbed. And she seemed so *shocked.*'

She looked over to where the Countess was talking urgently to her husband with her head bowed. Then she saw the Count shoot a sideways glance towards them. He took his wife's elbow and steered her across the room to a couple Violet recognised from the night of his win at the casino.

'I think I need some fresh air,' said Violet suddenly. 'We'll be sitting down to dinner in ten minutes. Then I'll be stuck for hours.'

Garth looked at Violet. He knew her well enough to understand that she was shaken. Perhaps she was right. It *was* hot and stuffy in the room and a dose of fresh air might sort her out. 'Be careful,' he said quickly.

'Don't you worry about me,' said Violet. She patted her lumpy satin bag. 'Toto will watch out for me.'

Five minutes later, Violet was standing with her hands on the ship's rail staring out at a sky the colour of flames and a sea that looked like molten silver. A sweet smell of pine trees and honey wafted over the water from the land. Then there was another smell, more sickly. Jasmine perhaps. It seemed very strong so far out at sea.

She leaned further over the rail, and let the breeze ruffle the skirts of her lawn dress and flutter her hair around her face.

For the first time that day she felt at peace and for a few minutes she let her mind drift with the sea.

Then there was the distant sound of a gong. Violet pushed her hair back from her face and whistled for Toto. It was time to go in for dinner. The tables had seating plans and Violet was sitting between the Baron and Garth. Lily had made sure she wouldn't have to talk to the Count and Countess for the rest of the evening.

Violet bent down to pick up her satin bag and whistled once more for Toto. Where *was* the silly dog?

Suddenly strong hands encircled her hips and lifted her high over the railings. Then the hands lowered her over the side and let go. It happened so quickly, Violet was too stunned to struggle or even cry out.

The next moment, she was falling headlong over the side of Frank Winalot's yacht.

TWELVE

At first, Violet had the sensation that everything was happening slowly. Then she hit the water with a hard *whack* and went straight under.

Instinct told her to keep her mouth shut and not scream, but even so her lungs were soon bursting. She rolled in the water and kicked off her satin pumps. Then she pushed herself upwards as fast as she could.

As soon as Violet broke the surface she screamed as loud as she could. But her voice came out as a thin squeak. The sides of Frank's yacht rose impossibly high. Even as she looked up, the yacht seemed further away and soon it had left her completely behind.

Violet stopped screaming and forced herself to think. She was a strong swimmer. The sea wasn't too cold, so she would probably be able to tread water for at least an hour. But a breeze was getting up and there was a small swell. Violet had the distinct impression that she was being blown out of the bay and towards the open sea.

She stared after the boat and waved her arms again. It was about a quarter of a mile away now and moving fast. She knew her only chance of rescue was if one of the crew spotted her in the water or if someone on board realised she was missing. She imagined the dining room crowded with people taking their places at the tables. Surely Garth would realise something was wrong when she didn't appear?

A sob rose in Violet's throat. If Garth *didn't* notice, she would surely drown. Suddenly the thought of never seeing her parents again made her shout with anger. She wasn't going to drown! And at that moment, something bobbing in the water caught her eye. Violet had no idea what it was, but it looked big and it floated. She turned and swam towards it.

It was an old barrel that had been used to store anchovies – rotten ones, by the smell of it. But to

Violet it was a miracle. She dragged herself onto the barrel and held on like a starfish. She ripped a length of fine lawn off her dress, thanking her lucky stars that she had chosen her light cream one, and tied herself onto two rings at either end of the barrel Then she lay her head down and began to paddle as well as she could towards the shore.

'Have you seen Violet?' Garth asked Lily as he made his way against a tide of chattering people pushing down the wide corridor from the drawing room to the dining room. He was suddenly aware that he hadn't seen her since she had decided to take a turn on deck, some twenty minutes earlier.

Lily shook her head. 'I thought she was with you.'

At that moment, Toto ran up to them, yapping. Garth picked him up and handed him to Lily. 'There's something wrong,' he said, his heart hammering in his chest. 'Could you put Toto in Violet's cabin and ask Frank to meet me on the foredeck? Don't run, though. No one must suspect a thing.'

Lily understood. If Count and Countess Drakensburg were the thieves, they still had time to steal the Baroness's diamonds and any kind of commotion might put them off. They had to be caught red-handed for the *gendarmes* to press charges.

Violet watched the setting sun with an unspeakable sadness. She was too tired to paddle any more and in twenty minutes it would be dark. She'd read somewhere that when you die, your life flashes before your eyes. But what do you do when you know you are going to die and there isn't much time left? She tried to remember the parts of her life she most cherished – sitting with her father in his study, talking about books; her pet monkey Homer, eating nuts out of her hand; meeting Garth for the first time and knowing within minutes that they would be friends for life; a cup of tea with her mother after a visit to a gallery. There were so many things to try and remember. And to think she had once believed there would be many more to come in the future.

A great shudder of grief passed through her. Violet let her legs dangle in the water and rested her head against the stinking wood of the barrel.

The moment Garth told him of Violet's disappearance, Frank gave orders to slow down the yacht and told his crew to search everywhere. Since all his guests were eating, no one noticed what was going on. When no trace of Violet could be found, they changed course towards the open sea. It was the direction the current would have taken Violet if she were still alive. Now, just as the sun was about to set, Frank, Garth and two crew members were standing on deck, scanning the water.

Garth stared desperately through his binoculars. It was hopeless. There was no sign of Violet. If only he'd gone with her on deck, none of this would have happened. He had seen that she was upset. He should never have left her alone.

Suddenly Frank saw her.

'There she is,' he cried. 'Over there! She's floating on something.'

Garth peered again through his glasses and felt a great lump in his throat. It was the pale yellow of Violet's skirt that made it possible to see her against the greyness of the water. If Violet had been wearing anything darker, they would never have found her.

'Tell the captain full steam ahead,' said Frank to the sailor at his side. As the man ran off, he turned to his white-coated steward. 'And you, Andrews, tell the band to play more loudly in the dining room. I don't want anyone noticing the change in the engine revs.' Then he went across to where his bathing suit was folded over the back of a chair and quickly changed into it.

Garth was pretty sure that so far no one had any idea what had happened. Earlier, Lily had spread the rumour that Violet had left the party after too many glasses of champagne, and that Frank had had to take her to her cabin to lie down.

The Baroness had frowned at the news. Violet had seemed such a sensible girl. And she was sure she had only been drinking lemonade. She told the Baron, who had seemed oddly agitated by the news but in the end agreed with her that perhaps the poor girl was suffering from too much sun.

Now Garth held onto the rail beside Frank, who stood in a towelling robe, waiting as the yacht edged closer to the figure which clung like a starfish over a wooden barrel. Neither of them spoke. Despite repeated calls across the water, Violet had not acknowledged them.

Garth stared stupidly down at the fine yellow fabric, spread out like wings on either side of Violet's lifeless body. He couldn't bring himself to think the terrible thought battering at the edge of his mind.

'Meet me at the stern with my steward,' said Frank, as he took off his robe and stood in his bathing suit. 'You can trust him.' Frank climbed over the rail and stood on the edge of the deck. 'And don't worry, she's not dead.'

'How do you know?'

'The angle of her neck. No corpse lies like that.' Frank touched Garth's shoulder. 'I'll wave from the water to tell you for sure. Then get a message to Lily.' Without waiting for a reply, Frank did a perfect swallow dive into the water.

Garth watched with his heart in his mouth as Frank swam up to the floating barrel. A second later, he turned in the water and waved his hand, thumb up, in the air.

Violet was alive!

Garth made his way quickly through the wide companionway and down into the main reception room, where the guests had been served champagne before dinner. White-coated servants were clearing glasses and plumping up feather cushions for the moment when the ladies would retire and leave the gentlemen

183

to their port and tobacco. Now Garth watched as a steward bent down and picked up a sheer purple stole that had fallen on the floor. Garth recognised it immediately. It belonged to the Countess Drakensburg. As he stared at it, an idea took shape in his mind.

'I'll return this to the Countess,' he said to the steward. 'I'm going to the dining room right now.'

As the steward handed over the stole, a particular perfume filled the air between them. It was the smell of jasmine.

A minute later, Garth walked past the glass doors of the crowded dining room. Voices roared over the *clink* of glass and the *clash* of cutlery. He had no intention of going in and was about to give a waiter a message for Lily, when she looked up and they exchanged the briefest of nods. Now she knew that Violet was safe, the rest of the plan should work out exactly as they had hoped. Violet and Garth's place settings had been removed and the young people's absence was already forgotten.

Garth ducked back into the corridor. He couldn't risk being seen. Then he went straight to his cabin, put the stole in his overnight bag and hurried back to the deck to see Frank swimming through the water with Violet held firmly in one arm.

Violet had no idea where she was when she opened her eyes. The walls were pale green, and long chintz curtains hung from two windows at the end of her bed. There was a round, button-backed chair covered in the same material as the curtains and a dressing table with two silver-backed brushes and a selection of tortoiseshell combs arranged on a glass top.

Violet eased herself up on her pillows and looked out of the windows. She saw a terraced hillside of olive trees. A chestnut horse with a white flash on its forehead was tethered in a small field in front of the house.

It was Tempest, the stallion she had ridden with Lady Caroline Egmont.

The door opened and Lady Caroline came into the room. 'Thank heavens,' she cried, crossing over to Violet's bedside. 'How do you feel, my dear? We've been so worried!'

'What happened to me?'

'Can't you remember? Oh dear! You must have hit your head.' Lady Caroline plumped up Violet's pillows. 'Frank says you slipped on the deck.' She sat down on a chair and gave Violet a glass of liquid. 'Drink this. The doctor said you should have it the moment you woke.'

Violet gulped at the drink. It was sweet and salty at the same time, and it made her feel better. She handed back the glass and leaned against the pillows. 'Where's Garth?' she asked.

'Downstairs in the drawing room,' replied Lady Caroline. 'He's desperate to see you but the doctor was quite adamant that you were to rest and not over-excite yourself.'

There was a tap on the door.

'Come in,' said Lady Caroline.

Garth walked into the room and immediately ran to Violet's side. 'Vi! How are you feeling? You nearly drowned!'

Lady Caroline clicked her tongue. 'Frank said the rails were too low.' She looked at Garth and said in a warning voice, 'The poor girl seems to have bumped her head. She can't remember how. And the doctor has said she must rest.'

'Oh,' said Garth in a vaguely disappointed voice.

'I'm feeling much better already,' said Violet, sens-

186

ing that Garth wanted to talk to her alone. 'Actually I'm as hungry as a horse.'

'I'll speak to Cook,' said Lady Caroline. 'But promise me you won't overdo things.'

'I promise.'

When the door shut, Garth slumped into the chair beside Violet's bed. 'You nearly drowned,' he said again in a hoarse voice. 'Did you really slip?'

Violet frowned. 'I don't think so. One minute, I was standing by the rails, the next I was falling over the side.' But even as she spoke, she knew she had left something out.

'What's this about the rails being too low?' asked Violet in a puzzled voice. 'They weren't. They had nothing to do with it. I was pushed!' The memory made her shiver with horror

'It was Frank's idea,' said Garth. 'When you dis-appeared before dinner we had to make sure no one knew, because there was still a chance an attempt would be made to steal the Baroness's jewels. So we put around a rumour that you drank too much champagne and went to bed. Then we told everyone you'd gone on deck for some fresh air and stumbled over the rails.'

'Because I was *drunk*?' said Violet.

'Exactly.'

'Whose idea was that?'

'Lily's,' said Garth. 'Clever, wasn't it?'

It was reasonably clever. But Violet found herself feeling annoyed that anyone could say such a thing about her. 'But surely whoever pushed me overboard must be wondering why we're trying to cover it up?'

'True. But at least the whole of Monte Carlo isn't talking about the attempted murder of Lady Violet Winters, so it might give us a little more time to catch the thieves.' Garth shrugged. 'Frank thinks so anyway.'

Suddenly there was the sound of raised voices outside the door.

'No! You cannot! Her Ladyship forbids it.' The maid's voice was high and agitated. But the voice that replied was almost hysterical.

'You, out of my way!' cried Marie. 'This is errand of emergency. I come all the way from Monte Carlo in secret travelling. I see my friend, now!'

At that moment, the door burst open and Marie Cherkassky exploded into the room. Her hair hung wildly about her face and she looked as if she had pulled on her dressing gown over trousers and a pair of stout boots.

When she saw Violet sitting propped up in bed, she let out a scream of anguish and threw herself down on her knees by her side. 'O my beloved friend! This is my fault! If only I meet you that night in the garden.'

Marie looked upwards and placed her hands together as if she was praying. 'But it was prevented by those demons! They poisoned me! I couldn't warn you.' She paused and pushed her face close to Violet's. 'I couldn't move. Death had me in his icy grab.'

Garth could feel his temper rising. The last thing they needed now was this crazy Russian. If she had something to tell them, fine. Otherwise, she could leave. He pulled up a chair and put it beside Violet's bed.

'Sit down, Marie,' he said firmly. 'Violet is still recovering. You must not upset her.' As he spoke, he practically manhandled the Russian girl into the chair and pushed her down. 'Now, tell us your message and for heaven's sake stop shouting.'

Marie stared at him for a moment, her mouth opening and shutting like a fish. No one had ever talked to her like that before. Perhaps it was the American way. Well, she would give her friend the benefit of the doubt. This time, anyway. She sat bolt upright on her chair and arranged her clothing as tidily as she could, given she *was* wearing a dressing gown over trousers.

'I am begging your forgiveness, Violet,' she said in a new, low voice. 'Now I tell you everything, for you are in great danger. This time perhaps you fall. Another time, I am saying, you are pushed.'

Violet went white as a sheet. 'How do you know this, Marie?'

'In the beginning, I begin,' replied Marie. 'And now I see from your face, you already have fear. So, I send you letter to meet me because I have a warning for you. Then flowers come from admirer with box of chocolates. I eat only two because the porpoise Tanenko steals them away.' Marie wiped a tear from her cheek. 'I owe my life to the porpoise. The chocolates were poisoned and I am very sick. So I cannot come to the gardens that night.' She sighed deeply. 'I am so sorry.'

'But what did you want to tell us?' asked Garth, sharply. 'What did you want to warn us about?'

Marie's eyes went round and dark. 'I am the gift of psychic,' she said, touching her forehead. 'I am feel-

190

ing all the badness from these Count and Countess and these other people.'

'The ones you met at the café with us?' asked Violet.

'Them.' Marie leaned forward in her chair. 'They are bad. But something else, strange. I cannot understand. So I use my mirrors to help you. It is Russian gift of psychic.' She closed her eyes and her voice dropped to a hoarse whisper. 'I stare and stare and finally I see but still I don't understand.'

Despite herself, Violet shivered. There was a strange feeling in the room. It was spooky and yet there was a sense of anticipation, as if something extraordinary was about to be revealed.

'What did you see in your mirrors?' asked Violet.

'Shadows,' replied Marie. Now she was rocking back and forth on her chair. 'Then the shadows lift, like misty shapes, and I see four people. I see those four people all together.'

Garth frowned. 'You mean the Duchamps and the Count and Countess?'

Marie nodded. 'All of them are bad.' She looked round at Garth. 'They are all together.'

Garth felt the hairs prickle on his neck. 'The porter at the Hermitage said the Duchamps arrived back late last night,' he said to Violet. 'After Frank's yacht tied up in the harbour.'

'And the Count and Countess?'

'They're at the hotel too, as far as I know.'

Garth picked up a small case that Violet hadn't noticed and put it on his knee.

'What's in that?'

'You'll see in a moment. It was Toto who gave me the idea when he ripped a piece out of Henri Duchamps's trousers.' Garth opened the case.

Violet and Marie found themselves staring at a sheer purple stole.

Marie picked up the stole and smelled it. 'Stinking jasmine reek,' she said. 'Only fake Russian would wear such stench.'

Violet's face went white. 'I've just remembered,' she said in a voice barely above a whisper.

'What?' asked Garth. He sat down beside her. 'What is it, Vi?'

'I smelled jasmine,' said Violet slowly. 'Just before somebody lifted me up and dropped me over the rails.'

Garth felt a shiver of excitement pass through him. 'Vi,' he whispered, 'we're going to get them this time, I'm sure of it.'

Violet stared at him. 'What do you mean?'

'I not understand either,' said Marie. She dropped the stole back into the suitcase. 'Why you want such filthy souvenir?'

Garth smiled as if he was the cat that had got the cream.

'The Countess was wearing that stole at the reception,' he said. He turned to Violet. 'Wasn't she?'

Violet nodded without speaking.

'And, as Marie says, jasmine is the perfume she always wears,' continued Garth.

At that moment, the sound of Thunder and Lightning, baying excitedly, came in through the window.

'Do you know what kind of dogs those are?' Garth asked Marie.

'Big, slobbery, droopy-eye beasts,' replied Marie with a shrug.

But Violet knew what he was thinking and she could feel her body begin to tingle with excitement.

Garth grinned at the look on her face and turned back to Marie. 'They're bloodhounds, Marie. They can track down anything if they have a scent to follow.' He pointed to the suitcase. 'That stole, stinking of jasmine, is just what they need.'

Marie frowned. 'I not understand. If you think fake Russians is thieves, why you not tell *gendarmes* to search their room?'

'Because we can't find out where either the Duchamps or the Drakensburgs are staying in the hotel,' explained Garth. 'They've probably bribed the porter. For all I know, the Duchamps smuggled themselves onto Frank's yacht, threw Vi overboard, then used the smell of jasmine to set up the Countess.' He paused. 'If it *is* the Duchamps.'

Now Violet sat up in bed and turned excitedly to Marie. 'So, if we use the dogs to track down the scent, we'll find the room and the thieves, and I'm almost certain the diamonds will be hidden there, too.'

'At any rate,' said Garth, 'the bloodhounds are our last chance, because I'll bet my bottom dollar both the Duchamps and the Drakensburgs will disappear any day now.'

Suddenly Marie stood up. 'I go,' she said abruptly. Then, for the first time, her voice went quiet, her face serious. 'But you remember this, my English friends. When the mysteries reveal at last, the danger is greatest.'

194

THIRTEEN

Madame Poisson smoothly folded the skirt of her new suit and packed it neatly beside a matching jacket. The outfit was beautifully tailored and made out of dove-grey linen edged with white, and the jacket was lined with scarlet silk. Madame Poisson had chosen the colours herself, and she was very pleased with them.

As she put the last of her belongings into a well-patched Gladstone bag, the little governess let her mind go back over the past week. It had been the most extraordinary week of her life. Madame Poisson still had no idea exactly what was going on in the Winters' household but at least she had the satisfaction of knowing she had carried out Lord Percy's instructions to the letter. No sooner had Lady Eleanor been robbed than Lord Percy had summoned Madame Poisson to his suite. He told her that he and Lady Eleanor were leaving that afternoon for a week's holiday in Italy. Then he said that the governess was to take the week as leave and move to a more comfortable hotel on the other side of Monte Carlo, where he had reserved her a room.

'But Your Lordship,' Madame Poisson had protested, 'who will look after Garth and Violette?'

Lord Percy had explained that their good friends Henri and Florence Duchamps would be the young people's guardians temporarily and that as Madame had not had a holiday for well over two years and it was known that she enjoyed the casino, he had decided it would be an excellent opportunity for her, from which everyone would benefit. Finally, he had asked her to ensure that during this time, she had no contact with Violet or Garth whatsoever. 'I cannot give you my reasons,' Lord Percy had said. 'But it must be as if you have disappeared from their lives for a week.'

Then Lord Percy had handed her a small envelope.

He had a proposition for her, he explained. He would be offended if she didn't accept it.

Madame Poisson opened the envelope and found herself staring at fifty thousand francs.

'*Mais, Monsieur! Je ne comprends pas!*'

'It's a wager, Madame,' Lord Percy had said. 'As you know, everyone is a gambler in this town and naturally Her Ladyship and I have made a bet between us.'

'A bet?' Madame Poisson repeated stupidly.

Lord Percy smiled reassuringly. 'Her Ladyship bets you will lose the money. I bet you will make ten times that amount. Will you assist us in this?'

Lord Percy could see from the angry flush on Madame Poisson's cheeks at Lady Eleanor's insult that she had taken the bait hook, line and sinker. Now at least the little French woman would be safely out of the way and, with her legendary skill at the card table, she might even have a chance of winning enough money to save her family farm. Lord Percy was well aware that Madame Poisson would never have accepted a gift or even a loan from him. Her pride would not have allowed it.

'But what shall I do with the money?' asked

Madame Poisson in an astonished voice. For it never occurred to her that she would lose.

'Spend it how you like, Madame.' Lord Percy raised his eyebrows and pushed the challenge home. 'Her Ladyship suggested you might enjoy a new outfit.'

Madame Poisson stiffened imperceptibly, thanked her employer and left the room, vowing at the same moment to turn the fifty thousand francs into five hundred thousand.

It was exactly the reaction Lord Percy had been hoping for.

Now, as Madame Poisson did up the leather straps of her case, she looked at the neatly packed trunk in the corner of the room. One new outfit? She had bought herself an entire new *wardrobe*, three new pairs of boots, four hats, a brand-new Singer sewing machine and a subscription to a catalogue containing all the latest patterns. Not only that, she had wired three hundred thousand francs to her Uncle Hugo in Paris. The money would cover the outstanding bank loan on the family farm, pay for a new well and mend the roof. A further ten thousand francs had been set aside for new fencing and livestock.

Madame Poisson had achieved her dearest wish. Les Pradelles was safe. She could also repay Lord Percy's original wager and still have enough money left over to open a savings account for herself.

The truth was that Madame Poisson need never work again. She had turned the fifty thousand francs into five hundred thousand francs and she was so pleased with herself she could have whistled in the street!

There was a knock and the door opened.

A maid bobbed. 'Your cab is waiting, Madame.'

The little French governess looked out of the window. It was a bright, warm day and the Hermitage was barely a mile away. 'Send it on with my things,' she said.

Madame Poisson decided to walk down the promenade in the sunshine.

And, if no one was about, she would jolly well whistle!

'You sure you're feeling strong enough?' Frank Winalot asked Violet two days after Marie's visit. It was the first time Violet had seen him since falling overboard.

'I'm fine, Frank,' said Violet. 'I promise.' She grinned. 'In fact, I'm really, really bored! And I almost forgot, I owe you a huge thank-you for saving my life.'

'My pleasure,' said Frank, smiling in return. 'I owe you a huge apology for letting murderous thieves onto my yacht.' He paused. 'Whoever they are.' Then his face went serious. 'This time, they're not going to get away from us.'

After Garth had explained to Frank his idea of using the dogs to track down the true thieves and the haul of diamonds, the plan had moved along swiftly. Lady Caroline had been consulted and agreed to lend Thunder and Lightning on the condition that no harm would come to them. After Frank pledged his life and fortune on the dogs' well-being, he immediately put out word that the Baron and Baroness were returning to Paris in two days' time.

'That should put the cat among the pigeons,' he explained to Garth and Violet. 'One of them's bound to make a move.'

Now Violet stood beside Frank's pink Bentley convertible and watched as Lady Caroline crossed her white gravel drive with the two bloodhounds pulling at their leads.

'Honestly, Frank,' she protested at the sight of the Bentley. 'Can't you do better than this? Thunder and Lightning are not at all used to open motor cars.'

'My other one's a Rolls,' said Frank with a shrug. 'And that's a rag top, too. Heck, Your Ladyship, if it's the upholstery you're worried about, Lily wants to change the colour anyway.'

Frank opened the pink door and Thunder and Lightning jumped in as if they had ridden in convertibles all their lives.

Garth clambered into the back and Violet sat in the front.

Lady Caroline clapped her hands delightedly. 'You two look simply wonderful!' she cried.

Garth nudged Violet in the back and they both burst out laughing.

It was perfectly obvious that the old lady was talking to her dogs.

Half an hour later, as Madame Poisson walked along the seafront, the roar of a pink convertible interrupted her whistling. The little governess looked up just in time to see her dear Violette sitting in the front and Garth, in between two bloodhounds, sitting in the back. For a split second, Madame Poisson stared. Then she remembered her agreement with Lord Percy. Then again, her week away from Violet and Garth was over. She hitched up her skirts and began to run.

Frank turned up a side street well before the hotel and stopped the car on a patch of waste ground. If the plan was going to work, they had to have surprise on their side.

Violet climbed out of the front. Now that everything was coming to a head, she was almost dancing from foot to foot with excitement.

'Ready for this?' Garth was trying to look controlled and responsible, but he was just as excited as she was.

'Never readier,' said Violet.

Behind them, Frank was struggling to keep Thunder and Lightning under control. Apart from all the new smells around, both hounds had picked up on the excitement and were running about with their noses glued to the ground.

'What will we do if they've left the hotel?' asked Garth.

Frank shook his head. 'They'll be there.'

*

Five minutes later, Garth and Violet walked up the wide stone steps to the Hermitage Hotel. Once they had confirmed that the Duchamps and the Count and Countess were still there, they would meet Frank on the promenade, where he was waiting with Thunder and Lightning. Then they would let the dogs smell the Countess's stole. After that, it was up to Garth and Violet to follow the hounds and see where they led them, while Frank joined the other guests in the drawing room. If either the Duchamps or the Drakensburgs were there, his job was to keep them busy.

'I can't come with you and the dogs,' Frank had explained. 'I don't like it, but the truth is if anything goes wrong, my cover as a millionaire playboy –' he grinned sheepishly – 'will be blown apart. And then I'd be useless if the agency ever needed my help again.'

'Don't worry,' Garth had replied. 'We're used to being accused of childish pranks. Aren't we, Vi?'

'Happens all the time,' said Violet, grinning. 'We're only children, anyway.'

'OK, OK,' said Frank. 'Don't rub it in. Just remember, once you go in with the dogs, you'll only have a few minutes.' He gave them a long look. 'And be careful. Anything could happen.'

Garth felt for the heavy penknife he had put in his pocket at the last moment. The same thought had occurred to him.

'I'm sorry,' said the manager as Garth and Violet waited by the front desk of the hotel. 'The Duchamps left first thing for Paris and the Count and Countess took the eleven o'clock train to Berlin.'

Violet couldn't hide her disappointment.

'Did you have an appointment with them, Mademoiselle?' asked the manager kindly. He looked under the polished walnut counter to see if any messages had been left. 'No messages – apart from this one from the Baroness Orzo. I am asked to advise her if I see you.'

'Are the Baron and Baroness in the hotel right now?' asked Garth.

'Why, of course. They are in the drawing room with the Van de Kaas from Rotterdam.' The manager stepped out from behind the counter. 'Shall I tell the Baroness you are here?'

'No, thank you,' said Violet, struggling to keep her voice steady.

'As you wish, Mademoiselle.'

Garth and Violet walked down to the end of the entrance hall and through a pair of French windows into the garden. The mimosa trees were covered with yellow blossom and the air was heavy with their scent.

Violet sat down on a wrought-iron bench and stared at her hands. 'We'll never track either of them down now. Frank was wrong – whoever they are, they must have decided it was too risky to hang on for the Baroness's diamonds.'

'It's my fault,' said Garth, as if to himself. 'As soon as I told Frank about the stole, he wanted to bring in the bloodhounds right away.'

'But you waited for me to get better,' said Violet miserably. She got up. 'There's another door out of the garden. We might as well go that way and tell Frank.'

Garth didn't reply. He was standing still as a statue behind the mimosa tree, looking in at the drawing room. 'Snakes alive!' he cried. 'I've been so stupid. So incredibly stupid!'

Violet froze. 'What are you talking about? What can you see?'

Garth stepped back. 'Look at the far end of the room on the right-hand side. There's a table by the fireplace. The Baron and Baroness are there with that Dutch couple the manager mentioned.'

'So?'

'Look at the Dutchman's hands!'

Violet moved carefully forward, making sure she couldn't be seen behind the mimosa, and peered in the window. The Baron was talking to a blond-haired man with thick glasses. The Baroness was sitting next to a woman dressed in an ugly tweed outfit with a blotchy face and a lopsided bun.

The Baron was holding a copy of a Paris newspaper and pointing at the front page.

'See?' whispered Garth.

Violet looked really hard. Then her heart banged in her chest!

The Dutchman was drumming his fingers on his lapel.

'Just like Henri Duchamps on the train,' whispered Violet to Garth.'

'And the Countess's chauffeur at the Riviera

Palace,' said Garth. 'And look at his face.'

Violet stared at the Dutchman and suddenly she saw the pinched expression of Henri Duchamps and the weasel-like glitter of Count Drakensburg's eyes.

Violet stepped back. 'It's them! They're both the same people!'

She almost whooped with glee. 'And they're just too greedy to leave without stealing the Baroness's diamonds!'

'Come on,' said Garth. They began to walk quickly towards the garden door. 'If we hurry, we'll catch them red-handed!'

FOURTEEN

'I know this is a silly question, Frank,' said Garth, 'but when do they start baying? While they're looking for the trail? Or after they've found it?'

'How should I know?' said Frank, as he handed over the leads to Garth and Violet. 'The only certain thing is that they'll take you to the room where there's a smell of jasmine. But like I said, be careful. I've sent for the *gendarmes*. Once these guys realise they're trapped they could get nasty.'

'Don't worry,' said Garth. 'We won't do anything stupid.'

'Glad to hear it.' Frank put the case on the ground. 'Are you ready?'

Violet looked sideways at Garth. 'Go!' they said together.

Frank kicked open the suitcase with the stole inside. Thunder and Lightning pushed their snouts inside and took off like tornadoes, baying at the tops of their voices.

'*Bon Dieu!*' shouted the hotel manager, rushing out from behind his desk. 'Get these—' but he never finished his sentence. Thunder and Lightning knocked him flat, leaving muddy footprints on his snowy-white coat as they clambered over him and cantered up the stairs.

'Hold on,' gasped Garth as they were dragged up another flight of stairs. 'If the dogs get away from us, we'll never find the room or the diamonds in time.'

Violet thought her arm was going to come out of its socket. 'How long have we got?' she shouted.

'They'll know we're here now,' shouted Garth over the baying of the bloodhounds. 'As long as Frank can keep them in the drawing room!'

In the drawing room, Frank Winalot was putting on a brilliant act as he apologised for the disturbance caused by his bloodhounds. 'It's all my wife's fault,' he insisted. 'I gave the dogs to her for her birthday and she insists on taking them with her everywhere, as if they were, uh, toy poodles!'

A ripple of amused laughter went around the room and for a moment Frank thought that he might be able to play for a little more time.

Then the Dutchwoman suddenly jumped up, let out an ear-piercing scream and fell to the ground. At the same moment, an enormous vase of flowers crashed onto the floor.

Pandemonium broke out. Chairs and tables were knocked over as all the guests jumped up at the same moment. When Frank looked again, the French doors were open. In the chaos, both the so-called Van de Kaas had disappeared.

Thunder and Lightning snuffled along a corridor on the fifth floor and stopped abruptly outside a room with a green door. They stood on their hind legs and scratched and howled louder than ever.

Violet looked at the card fitted into a small frame. It said in French, *M. & Mme. Van de Kaas do not wish to be disturbed.*

Violet tried the handle. 'It's locked,' she said, gasping for breath.

'Not for long.' Garth reached into his trouser pocket and took out his penknife. He fitted it between the door and the frame and pushed it hard to one side. There was the sound of splintering wood and the door swung open.

Thunder and Lightning rushed inside, made a single circuit of the room and stuck their snouts into an open wardrobe. Lightning pulled out the dress the Countess had worn on Frank's yacht and dragged it to the floor. Then, baying at the tops of their voices, they took off down the corridor again.

Neither Garth nor Violet called them back. One look around the room told them the bloodhounds had done their job.

'Holy mackerel,' murmured Garth.

The room was shadowy because the curtains were pulled. But even in the gloom, they could make out half a dozen dressmakers' dummies. Outfits Violet remembered well hung on each one.

There was the tailored suit that Florence Duchamps had worn on the boulevard in Paris; there was the yellow gown trimmed with lace that the Countess had worn at dinner in the Ritz with Mrs Stuyvesant Fish. Beside it was the Count's evening dress jacket and beside that Henri Duchamps' loud, check suit.

Wigs that now looked horribly familiar sat on wooden moulds on a table against the wall.

Violet stared first at Florence Duchamps's short blonde bob, then at the Countess's dark red curls.

In the far corner was a chauffeur's uniform.

'How could we have been so *stupid*?' asked Violet, as she picked up Florence Duchamps's bright red beret and held it beside the cluster of jewelled ostrich feathers the Countess had worn at the casino. 'It's been staring us in the face all this time.'

'We didn't see it because we weren't looking for it,' said Garth simply.

He opened a flat leather box and saw the Count's moustache and a beard. 'Frank didn't see it. Neither did your father or the Baron or anyone else who's tried to catch them.'

Garth turned to Violet. 'And remember, we still don't know their real names.'

But Violet wasn't listening. She desperately wanted to find her mother's engagement ring before the *gendarmes* arrived and confiscated everything in the room.

Where would the thieves have hidden it?

Violet let her head fill with all the disguises and play-acting and cheating and lying that been going on since that first moment on the boulevard when she had been drinking hot chocolate and eating *petits fours*. Somehow, out of all the disguises, she felt sure the one nearest to the *real* person – whoever that was – was the character of Florence Duchamps. The whole scam was clever and modern and almost stylish. Violet picked up a silver letter opener from the desk and walked over to the dummy dressed in the tailored suit. Then she ripped off the black fitted jacket and plunged the silver blade into the dummy's canvas and straw body.

Garth spun around. 'What are you doing?' Then he shut his mouth and stared in amazement. Behind the canvas skin and set into the packed straw in the dummy's back was a wooden drawer with a metal handle. He tugged the handle hard and the drawer shot out.

Glittering jewellery fell all over the floor.

Violet watched as her mother's emerald and diamond engagement ring rolled over and over. She bent down and picked it up.

'Put that back,' said a thin voice behind them.

Violet spun round, clutching the ring in her hand. It was impossible to tell whether the man who stood in front of them was Henri Duchamps or Count Drakensburg or the Dutchman from Rotterdam. The only certain thing was that he was pointing a pistol straight at them.

'What a pity you didn't drown, Lady Violet,' said the man in a conversational tone of voice. 'In fact, you have both become rather a nuisance.'

'You won't get away this time,' said Garth angrily. 'The *gendarmes* have been called. Your wife will be arrested by now.'

'Who said she was my wife?' replied the man with a nasty smile. Then his expression changed and he waved the gun in Violet's face. 'Sit down on that chair. And you –' he turned to Garth – 'tie her up.'

As the man turned his attention to Garth, Violet saw Madame Poisson appear in the doorway. It didn't even occur to her wonder how on earth her dear cod-fish had found them. Violet only noticed that the little governess was holding a new parasol upside down so that the solid china handle could be used as a club. Violet decided that the best way to distract the man's attention was to make him angry. Then it was just possible that the presence of Madame Poisson and her heavy china parasol handle might prove enough of a surprise to give them a chance to knock the pistol out of his hand and overcome him.

It was their only hope.

'No one ties me up,' cried Violet in her haughtiest voice. She stamped her foot on the floor. 'Don't you know who I am, you pathetic little crook?'

'Violet!' cried Garth, his eyes nearly popping out of his face. 'He has a gun. Don't be crazy!'

It was exactly as Violet had hoped. Garth was completely taken aback, which could only help to put the man off his guard.

Now she had to make him believe that she and Garth were arguing for real and pray that Madame understood what she was up to. 'You're not going to do what this filthy impostor is asking, are you?' snarled Violet at Garth. 'Coward!'

Madame Poisson stepped forward silently.

'Shut up, you brat,' yelled the man. He turned to Garth. 'I said, tie her up!'

'No!' shouted Violet. 'No! No! No!'

'Do you want to get us killed?' said Garth angrily. He reached out towards her.

'Take your dirty hands off me,' shouted Violet. '*Now!*'

In that instant, Madame Poisson lifted up her parasol and thwacked the man she knew as Henri Duchamps as hard as she could on the back of his head.

The gun dropped from the man's hand and he fell forward. In the same moment Garth jumped on top of him and Violet grabbed a heavy glass paperweight and clobbered him over the ear. There was a deep groan, then he lay quiet.

Madame Poisson stood stock still, her arm raised to deliver another blow. 'Ooh la la, Violette,' she murmured. Then slowly she staggered backwards and passed out on the huge four-poster bed.

Violet bent down and picked up the engagement ring that she had dropped as she grabbed the paper-weight. She made sure her codfish wasn't hurt, then she went over to where Garth was standing, getting his breath back. She looked down at the man on the floor. 'Do you think he's dead?'

Garth shook his head and a small smile flickered

across his face. 'Nah. Just sleeping. But that was some show you put on. Congratulations.'

Violet smiled back. 'Thanks. You were pretty quick on your feet, too.'

Garth shook his head. 'I don't understand. How did flatfish know we were here?'

Violet shrugged. 'Your guess is as good as mine. But I'd say we'll find out soon enough.' She prodded the man with her foot. 'What shall we do with *what'shisname?*'

'Tie him up,' said Garth, taking the cord from a dressing gown that was slung over a chair. 'If you remember, it was *his* idea in the first place.'

Violet tied the man's ankles, while Garth bound his wrists behind his back.

It was a neat job and they both stepped back to admire it.

'Holy smoke!' Frank Winalot stood in the doorway, looking around the room, totally incredulous. 'Where are the *gendarmes?*'

'What *gendarmes?*' asked Violet.

'You mean they never arrived?' spluttered Frank.

Violet shook her head. 'I haven't seen any.' She turned. 'Have you, Garth?'

'Nope.'

Frank looked down at the body on the floor. 'You mean *you two* did that?'

Violet pointed to the four-poster bed, where Madame Poisson was lying. 'Madame bopped him on the head with the handle of her parasol, Garth jumped on him and I finished him off with a paperweight.'

Frank's eyes travelled to the gun that was lying under a chair. He groaned and put his head in his hands. 'What am I going to tell your father? This wasn't how we'd planned it at all.'

'Tell him what you like,' said Violet firmly. She grinned at Frank. 'But I have to say, it can't have been a very good plan, since I nearly drowned and now both of us could be riddled with bullets.'

Frank groaned again. 'OK, OK. Let's just say I owe you one!'

Violet went over and put her arms around the big American. 'You don't owe us anything, Frank. It's the other way around. You trusted us to do the job and we did it.'

Frank shook his head. 'Yeah. You're right. I should have listened to Mrs Stuyvesant Fish. She warned me about you two.'

'Oh, come on, Frank,' said Violet, in her best American accent, 'don't go soft on us now!' She smiled into his worried face. 'Here, give us a hand with my governess or there really *will* be trouble!'

'For heaven's *sake*, Percy,' cried Lady Eleanor, as she lay sprawled on a chaise longue in the drawing room of her suite. 'This hotel has gone completely mad! *Do* something!'

The moment Lady Eleanor had stepped through the front door, instead of being welcomed and escorted upstairs, she had, in her own words, been practically *trampled* by a gaggle of *gendarmes* who were rushing about like so many addled geese. And when she had turned to remonstrate with her husband, he had disappeared into the garden to have a long conversation with Frank Winalot!

Lady Eleanor sighed. Americans were all very well, but there was a time and a place for everything and now was neither the time nor the place for Frank Winalot to be gabbling like a baboon and waving his hands in the air. There was only one thing to do. Lady Eleanor retired to her suite and instructed her maid to pull the curtains and make up a cold compress. She was just about to lie down when there was a knock on the door and Violet walked into the room with Garth and Lord Percy.

Lady Eleanor could tell immediately that something was up. But with all the hullabaloo, she was not entirely sure she was interested enough to let that something interfere with her rest. Nevertheless, she hadn't seen her daughter for over a week now and Lady Eleanor decided she must make an effort.

'Darling,' she cried, taking in the fact that Violet's hair looked like a haystack and her blouse wasn't properly tucked into her skirt. 'You look a complete *mess*! What *have* you been doing?'

Lady Eleanor turned to Lord Percy. 'Why on earth you had to let that little governess loose in the casino for a whole week with fifty thousand francs, when she should have been looking after Violet, I shall never know!'

For the first time ever, Violet saw that her father was annoyed by his wife's indiscretion. His arrangement with Madame Poisson was obviously something Violet was not supposed to know about.

Violet stared at her father and felt a huge surge of affection wash over her. So *that* was the reason

Madame Poisson had looked so delighted when she came out of the casino! She must have won enough money to save Les Pradelles. Only her father would have understood that her codfish would never accept an outright gift and he knew she was a skilful card player. What a genius he was!

Lady Eleanor sat up on the chaise longue, aware that the attention had shifted way from her. 'Darling,' she said pettishly to Violet, 'shall we meet up later and compare adventures, then? I'm really rather weary after our journey.'

'Of course, Mother,' said Violet. 'There is just one thing I wanted to give you.' She reached into her pocket and held out the emerald engagement ring.

Lady Eleanor was thunderstruck. She looked from one face to another for an explanation, but when there was none to be had, she gave up and instead surrendered to the feeling that was building up inside her.

She shrieked with delight and snatched the ring from Violet's hand. 'My ring! My ring!' she cried, like a child. 'Darling! Where on earth did you find it?'

'In a dressmaker's dummy, Mother,' said Violet.

'I beg your pardon?'

'It's a long story,' replied Violet.

Lord Percy caught his daughter's eye and she smiled at him. He would know something of what had happened from Frank, but not everything. Perhaps one day she would tell him. Or perhaps she wouldn't.

Now they all watched as Lady Eleanor happily twisted her ring round and round on her finger and clucked over it like a broody hen.

Lord Percy cleared his throat quietly and suddenly Lady Eleanor recovered her poise. She stood up and kissed Violet on both cheeks.

'Thank you for finding my ring, darling,' she cried. 'You have *no idea* how much it means to me.'

Lady Eleanor stepped back and pushed a strand of hair off Violet's face. 'By the way, there's something waiting for you in your room. I hope you like it.'

'Thank you, Mother.'

'No, thank *you*, darling! Thank you so much.'

Now that her ring was back on her finger, it was as if Lady Eleanor had found herself again. She looked around the room and beamed. 'Cocktails at seven?'

Violet stared at her reflection in the long gilt-edged mirror and smoothed down the sapphire-blue evening dress her mother had ordered from Rome. For the first time, Lady Eleanor had thought of her daughter's tastes rather than her own. The dress was simple and elegant.

Beside her, Madame Poisson undid the clasp of an exquisite Lalique necklace of green enamel and polished lapis lazuli set in gold. It was an asymmetrical design in the new style and Violet loved it.

'*C'est beau*,' said the little governess as she fixed the necklace around Violet's neck. 'Lord Percy is very generous.'

'Yes.'

Violet suddenly turned and gave her dear codfish a hug. 'Thank you,' she said. 'I don't know what would have happened if you hadn't found us.'

'It was because of the big pink car and those nasty dribbling 'ounds,' said Madame Poisson. 'I ran when I saw you with them.' She put her finger to her lips. 'But all that is a secret now. We promised Monsieur Winalot.'

'Yes.'

Violet thought back to the hurried conversation with Garth and Frank Winalot before the hotel filled up with *gendarmes*. She knew it was the last one they would ever have with Frank about the whole affair.

'Their real names are Pierre and Cara Mageaux,' Frank told them quickly. 'They're trained actors, experts in disguise, ruthless thieves and wanted in just about every country in Europe.'

'Is there enough evidence to convict them?' Garth asked.

'Plenty,' said Frank. 'And it's all thanks to you guys. You put two and two together.' Frank shrugged. 'Maybe you should go professional one day. Uh, when you're twenty-one, that is.'

Violet raised her eyebrows and turned to Garth. 'You planning to wait that long?'

'Never,' replied Garth firmly.

Frank could only smile and shake his head.

Now, as Madame Poisson put the finishing touches to Violet's hair, her mouth was working in her face as if she was trying to make a decision. 'There is another secret,' she said at last. 'A happy secret. Les Pradelles is safe.'

'Oh, Madame!' cried Violet, knowing that her governess would never ever tell her the real story. 'I am so very glad for you. That is wonderful news.'

At that moment, there was a knock and the door

opened. Garth was standing in the corridor, wearing a white collar and tail coat.

'Vi!' he said breathlessly. 'I've been sent up to fetch you! Mrs Stuyvesant Fish has arrived and Marie is going to give us a special recital. Everyone is waiting for you!'

Violet looked at him, her eyes wide. 'I don't believe it!' she cried. Then she hitched up her elegant silk evening dress and raced down the corridor.

Violet sat between Garth and Mrs Stuyvesant Fish, watching as a Marie she had never seen before walked sedately up to a grand piano, bowed, then sat down and began to play.

Within moments, it was as if the entire room had been transported to another world. Violet stared at her Russian friend and felt pride surge through her. Marie was indeed a prodigy. Violet had never heard such beautiful playing in all her life. What's more, she could tell from the enthusiastic approval that radiated from Mrs Stuyvesant Fish as she watched Marie bent over the piano that the young Russian's money worries would soon be over.

'Superb,' murmured Mrs Stuyvesant Fish, half to

herself, as Marie finished her recital and bowed. 'Absolutely *superb.*' She turned to Violet. 'Do you think your young Russian friend would like New York?'

Before Violet could reply, Marie rushed over and grabbed her hands. 'My heart is bursted, dearest Violet! Bursted with joy!' She turned to Mrs Stuyvesant Fish and beamed. 'Who have thought, Mrs Empire State Building, that I, poor Russian girl, have such luck in acquaintance on the boulevard?' She turned back to Violet and kissed her heartily on both cheeks. 'It is a wondrous thing, is it not?'

'Exceedingly excellent, my dear,' cried Mrs Stuyvesant Fish, her face bright with laughter. She took Marie by the arm. 'Now, come with me.' Mrs Stuyvesant Fish winked at Violet. 'As New York's tallest building, I have something rather important to discuss with you.'

'I no understand,' replied Marie. She smiled happily at the huge woman with a vast bosom covered in pearls who was steering her into a corner of the room.

'You will, my dear,' said Mrs Stuyvesant Fish firmly. 'You will.'

'Champagne, pardner?'

Garth appeared at Violet's side carrying two fluted glasses filled to the brim and handed her one.

Violet took the glass and they both looked around the room. Everyone was laughing and talking and there was a real feeling of celebration in the air.

'Here's to ya,' said Violet in her best American accent. She raised her glass and smiled at Garth. 'Ya done great.'

'Thanks,' replied Garth, ignoring Violet's terrible accent. 'You were pretty good yourself.' He smiled and held up his own glass. 'So, what would you say are the chances of us having another adventure soon?'

Violet laughed as the cold bubbles slid down her throat. 'I'd put money on it!'

IF YOU ENJOYED *DIAMOND TAKERS*, LOOK OUT FOR LADY VIOLET'S NEXT MYSTERY ADVENTURE, *SNOW SHADOWS*, COMING SOON! HERE'S AN EXTRACT . . .

"So, what do you know about the people we are staying with?" asked Garth as he sat with Violet on a stuffed leather seat in the back of the shiny black sledge waiting outside the station at St. Petersburg. In front of them, the driver of the other sledge handed Lady Eleanor up the step and tucked a vast woollen rug lined with fur around her knees.

Violet watched as the last of her parents' luggage was strapped to the back and her father settled in beside her mother. "I don't know a lot about them," she said to Garth. "They're an old banking family but you wouldn't call them aristocrats. I mean, they haven't got titles or anything but when Ivan Rahl comes to London, he always stays at Claridges. The last time, Father dined with him there."

When Garth didn't reply, Violet saw that he was staring at the two sledge drivers who stood bundled up in sheepskin coats tied round with leather cords. They were waving their arms in the air and shouting about something. Garth leaned forward to catch what he could of their conversation. "They're arguing about the fastest route back to the Rahls' house," he explained.

Violet watched as the coachmen suddenly stopped shouting at each other and began to laugh. "What are they saying now?"

"They've made a bet over who gets there first," said Garth. He turned to Violet and grinned. "Looks like we'll have an exciting ride."

Twenty minutes later, Violet felt her heart pounding with excitement as their sledge whizzed over the hard, powdery snow. The metal runners hardly made any noise at all so it seemed as if they were flying through air that shimmered with ice crystals and sunshine.

"It's *incredible!*" cried Garth at the top of his voice. "Look!" He pointed to a wide river where ships were trapped like great black beetles in the dirty uneven ice.

Violet stared down the frozen white pathway which was the River Neva. Even if she couldn't understand Russian very well, she had memorized a map of the city so she knew that this part was separated into sections by three crescent-shaped canals which ran parallel to each other and emptied into the Neva. At that moment, the sledge driver turned left along the innermost canal and right over a humped back bridge across the second one. Now they were on a wide street lined with high buildings, each decorated with columns and porticos and painted in pale greens and blues and brick reds. Violet had seen such colours in cities like Venice and Florence but the scale of these buildings was enormous and, with their elaborate stonework and white painted detail, they reminded her of gigantic square wedding cakes. In fact, everything about St. Petersburg was huge. From the wide frozen river to the great domed churches that glittered gold in the sun. Even the statues on the street corners rose into the air like gigantic chess pieces.

Suddenly their driver cracked his whip in the air as if throwing down a challenge to his companion in front. Violet saw her parents' driver turn around and there was a flash of white teeth in the depths of a bushy brown beard. Then their sledge slewed round a corner and everything changed. They were on a narrow street and Violet found herself staring up at dirty grey buildings like the tenement blocks she had seen in New York. It was as if they were in a different world. Here the colours were drab and dirty and where before she had seen men in long beaverskin coats strutting purposefully down the pavements, now she saw beggars and women wrapped in ragged shawls with heavy loads slung over their backs.

The sledge slowed down and instinctively Violet and Garth slid down in their seat. The openness of the sledge that had been exhilarating five minutes before now made them feel exposed and uneasy.

"Tell the driver to go back to the big roads," said Violet in a tight voice. "I don't like this."

Garth patted her arm. "Reading my mind," he replied reassuringly. "I was about to do just that."

But as Garth leaned forward and shouted, the sledge stopped abruptly and his voice was suddenly drowned by hundreds of others.

Ahead of them, a big crowd of people had

appeared out of an alleyway. They were chanting angrily and holding up a big banner. As they drew nearer, Violet could see that most of them were young men with hats pulled down over their faces or scarves wrapped in such a way that only their eyes could be seen. However, their clothes were not ragged. It was clear they weren't beggars. Violet remembered what Garth had said on the train about revolutionaries being teachers and writers and lawyers.

"What does the banner say?" she asked.

"*Freedom to speak. Freedom to write. Freedom to think,*" replied Garth. As he spoke, he felt his own fear disappear and anger take its place. "I think they're protesting because the government is trying to stop them from teaching the workers how to read and write."

"But why?" asked Violet. "How else can they learn?"

"They can't and the Tsar doesn't want them to. He's afraid that once they can read and understand what's really going on, they'll rise up against the government."

A stone whistled through the air in front of them and smashed into a window on the other side of the street.

In front of them, the driver's voice was hoarse and angry.

"He says, 'sit as far back as you can'," said Garth. He looked at Violet. "This is getting dangerous, Vi."

But Violet couldn't resist poking her nose above the sides of the sledge. "But these are the people we wanted to find out more about."

"Maybe we did," said Garth. "But they aren't going to take kindly to the likes of us. We look like the enemy to them."

"But I believe in everything on that banner," cried Violet, angrily.

"*I* know that," replied Garth. "But they don't. Think about it, Vi. This sledge has a crest on it. The driver's cap is the Rahls' household colours."

At that moment, the driver shook his fist in the air and shouted something at the crowd in front of him. Violet didn't have to hear a translation to guess what he was saying and suddenly she was furious. How dare this man swear at fellow Russians who were risking their lives for his freedom and others like him. Before Garth could stop her, she sat up in full view of the crowd.

Now the sledge was surrounded on all sides by

hundreds of men and a few women. They were still chanting but unlike the driver, they were not shaking their fists or yelling.

The driver swore again and suddenly one young man stopped and glanced up. At the same moment, his scarf slipped from his face and Violet found herself staring at a young man with high cheekbones and eyes as black as lumps of coal. Unlike the faces on either side of him, his own was rigid with fury. For a split second they looked at each other, then the young man turned and ducked back into the crowd.

"You don't understand!" cried Violet, desperately. "I agree with you! I am your friend!"

"For Heaven's sake, Vi," said Garth, as he pulled her back into the shelter of the cab. "No-one can understand a word you're saying and if your parents find out about this, they'll forbid us to go out on our own!"

Violet hunched into the leather seat and said nothing. She had seen the young man hesitate for a split second as she spoke. She was almost positive he had understood English. But Garth was right. They had to get to the Rahls' house as quickly as possible.

As for the driver, she was sure he would lose his job if anyone ever found out what had happened.

Sure enough, the sledge quickly lurched to the left, into what looked like a crack between two houses and turned out to be the narrowest of alleyways. Suddenly they changed worlds again. Now they were back in bright sunshine, whizzing down a wide street lined with blue and green and yellow painted houses where men in beaverskin coats walked purposefully along the pavement.

It was as if the dirty alleyway and crowd of chanting people had been a bad dream.